MURDER
in
Moreton

Eliza Thomson Investigates

Book 2

By

VL McBeath

Murder in Moreton
By VL McBeath

*

Editing services provided by Susan Cunningham (www.perfectpros-eservices.com)
Cover design: BookCoversbyMelody
(https://bookcoversbymelody.com)

ISBNs:
978-1-9999426-5-6 (Kindle Edition)
978-1-9999426-7-0 (Paperback)

Main category - FICTION / Historical Mysteries
Other category - FICTION / Crime & Mystery

Previous book in the
Eliza Thomson Investigates
series

Introductory Novella: *A Deadly Tonic*

Get your FREE copy of *A Deadly Tonic*
by signing up to my no-spam newsletter for further
information and exclusive content about the series.

Visit
https://www.subscribepage.com/eti-freeadt

Further details can be found at **www.vlmcbeath.com**

CHAPTER ONE

Eliza Thomson closed her eyes and rested her head on the back of the carriage trying unsuccessfully to suppress a grin. As the horses slowed to a walk, she straightened up again hoping her husband hadn't noticed. But who was she fooling? Of course he had.

"What's the matter with you?" he asked.

Smiling at his soft Scottish lilt, she placed a gloved hand on his. "Oh, my dear, I do hope you grow to love this place as much as I do. Just promise me that whatever happens in the next half an hour, you won't go scurrying back to London."

Archie studied her, his dark brown eyes causing her stomach to flutter as they always did when he looked at her that way. "Why would I do that?"

Eliza stared out of the left-hand window as the carriage approached the surgery. "Because our private lives will soon be a thing of the past. I must have seen at least half a dozen sets of curtains twitching as we drove down the street, and my guess is that before we can climb down from the carriage, Connie will be out in the street to meet us."

Archie's brow furrowed. "She's your oldest friend, you'll be pleased to see her, won't you?"

"Of course I will, I can't think of a better person to be living next door to, but the speed with which she greets us will show you how quickly news travels around here."

"It's hardly got far to travel, we'll be stopping outside her house. Besides, I expect she'll be glad of the company now she lives alone."

Eliza peered through the window to catch a glimpse of the small terraced cottage nestled alongside the village surgery. "She will although she's used to it by now. It's over two years since Mr Appleton died. Besides, this is Moreton-on-Thames, not London. Everyone knows everyone around here; it's difficult to be on your own even if you want to be."

Her husband squeezed her hand. "That's good then, isn't it?"

"I suppose so, for Connie at least, but I worry about you. After living in London for so many years, becoming part of such a close-knit, not to mention nosy, community will take some getting used to ... if you ever do."

"It was my decision to come if you remember. We wouldn't be here if I wasn't happy about it."

Before Eliza had a chance to respond the carriage came to a halt and an attractive woman wearing a navy bonnet over dark blonde hair hurried down the garden path to meet them. A smile highlighted the faint lines around her turquoise eyes.

"You're here!" Connie's eyes sparkled as the driver helped Eliza from the carriage. "I've been looking out of the window for you since two o'clock. What kept you? Your horse and carriage arrived over an hour ago."

Eliza laughed. "We couldn't come in our little carriage.

We had bags we wanted to bring ourselves, so one of the removal men drove it over for us. By the time we'd loaded everything up, we didn't leave London until ten. Then we had to stop in Richmond and join Father for luncheon. You should be thankful we're here already. It's not four o'clock yet. Is the kettle on?"

Connie raised a hand to her lips, stifling a gasp, but Eliza grinned. "Don't look so worried, I'm teasing. We sent word to Iris, our new maid, that we'd be here around this time. Will you join us?"

Eliza linked her arm through Connie's, but her friend hesitated as Archie appeared from the far side of the carriage.

"I'd love to, as long as I'm not intruding. Don't you and Dr Thomson want to get settled in first?"

"Of course you're not intruding, we won't be doing anything until we've had a cup of tea, will we, dear?"

Archie rolled his eyes at his wife. "You might not be but I'm sure I'll be able to find something to do." He extended his hand to Connie. "Good afternoon, Mrs Appleton. It's nice to see you again. It looks like the removal men are finished."

A smile lit up Connie's face. "They are, they left about half an hour ago. I imagine the maid will have everything unpacked."

"I doubt it," Eliza said. "Didn't you see the number of crates we had delivered? Now, come along. The sun might be bright, but it isn't warm. I need to get inside and you can bring me up to date with all the gossip."

The double-fronted, stone cottage with its neatly trimmed thatched roof sat behind a small, well-stocked garden. Archie opened the gate for the ladies before he directed the driver around the back of the surgery towards the stables. He arrived at the front door before they did.

"While you familiarise yourself with the house, I might as well get myself acquainted with the surgery," Archie said. "It won't be long before people start hammering on the door wanting to be seen."

Connie nodded. "There've been people calling for the last week asking when to expect you. I told them not to bother you for a few days yet."

"You're a love, thank you." Eliza patted Connie's hand before turning her attention to Archie. "If you don't want to join us, I'll ask Iris to make up a separate tray and bring it through to the surgery for you."

"There's no need for that. Give me ten minutes and I'll join you." Archie ushered them through the front door, but the sound of the church bells announcing four o'clock brought Eliza to a standstill.

"Good gracious, I don't remember them being so loud." She put her hands over her ears. "I hope they don't ring all through the night. The surgery must be a lot closer to the church than our old house, we could hardly hear them there."

Connie shook her head. "Because you were surrounded by so many trees at your other house, I shouldn't wonder. You'll get used to them soon enough, although the way things are going, they won't be ringing for much longer."

Eliza's forehead creased. "Why not?"

"The bell tower needs repairing and unless they can find the money to mend it, the bells will need to be stopped. We'll all miss them if that happens, nobody will know what time it is."

Eliza put an arm around her friend. "In that case, I won't

4

complain and hope they can raise the money. Now, let's get inside."

Iris met them at the door and directed Archie towards a narrow corridor on the right-hand side that led to the surgery; she then showed the ladies to the drawing room. A fire cast a welcome glow across the room and Eliza flicked her eyes over the dark wooden panelling while resting her hands on the back of one of the two green velvet settees positioned opposite each other on either side of the hearth.

"It's a nice enough room, but the house feels so much smaller than the one in London. It's to be hoped we're not expected to do much entertaining."

"Nice enough indeed." Connie seated herself on the settee facing her friend. "This is a lovely big room, especially in the summer when the early evening sun shines through the bay window. If you wanted bigger, you shouldn't have married a doctor. You know what your father thought of the idea."

Eliza feigned a swoon onto the empty settee, disturbing the chignon that sat beneath the rim of her hat. "Don't remind me, but Archie's worth it, don't you think? Even after all these years he's still handsome, only more distinguished with those flecks of grey in such dark hair."

Connie sighed. "You know he is."

"And the profession's becoming more respectable," Eliza continued. "At least that's one less thing for Father to complain about."

Connie scowled at her friend. "Your father doesn't complain, he's a lovely man and you wouldn't have him any other way. He's spoiled you terribly over the years. What have you ever wanted that you didn't get?"

"That cup of tea for one thing." Eliza pushed herself from the settee in time to help Iris through the door with a large tray laden with a selection of sandwiches and cakes, cups, saucers and a polished silver teapot. "Ah, here you are; my, that looks nice. Cook's obviously been busy."

"We wanted to give you a good welcome, madam. There's a letter here for you, too; the letter opener's on the tray." Iris indicated towards the delicate silver knife.

Eliza picked up the large Manila envelope. "Thank you for everything you've done these last few days Iris, and can you thank Cook for me too? I'll pop into the kitchen to see you both once Mrs Appleton's gone."

"Very well, madam." Iris finished pouring the tea before moving to the settee to plump up the cushions. "Will that be all?"

"Yes, thank you."

With a brief curtsey, Iris headed for the door.

"What have you got there?" Connie sat forward in her seat as Eliza sliced open the top of the envelope and turned to the last page to confirm the sender.

A grin brightened Eliza's face. "It's from the police in Oxford. Did you see the details in the paper about a murder they had several months ago?"

Connie gave an involuntary shudder. "I saw the headlines, but I don't share your delight in reading about murder. I'd have thought you'd have gone off it, too, after what happened in London."

Eliza grimaced. "Yes, don't remind me, but it's quite different when the story's written up in the newspaper."

"If you say so." Connie failed to look convinced. "Anyway, why are the police sending you a letter?"

"I wrote to give them some advice about the case. They hadn't even considered the idea that the murderer could be a woman and so I explained to them why I thought they should."

Eliza turned her attention to the letter before looking back at Connie, her grin turning into a broad smile. "I was right. They followed up the suggestions and last week found the woman in question. She's admitted everything."

"She has? Well, that's wonderful. How do you do it?"

Eliza shrugged. "The newspapers report everything in such detail it's easy to follow if you pay attention. If I think they've missed anything, or they hit a dead end, I write and tell them."

"Really?" Connie's eyes were wide.

"Really. They always write back and this isn't the first time they've told me how helpful I've been. I've a folder somewhere where I keep all the letters, although goodness knows where it is now." She turned full circle in the middle of the room but there was nothing but boxes. "Never mind, I must show this to Archie before I put it away. Not that he'll think anything of it, he's always telling me not to waste police time. It never occurs to him that I'm being helpful, even after everything I did for him in London."

"I'm sure he does."

Eliza flopped back onto the settee. "Well, he doesn't show it."

"He's letting you work with him in the surgery, isn't he? He wouldn't let you do that if he didn't think you'd be a help."

"You're right, but that's different." Eliza pouted. "It's probably his way of stopping me helping the police ... interfering he calls it. I didn't spend all that time studying

7

science at Bedford College to sit and do nothing. That's why I love keeping up with the murder cases. It keeps my mind active. Not that Archie understands."

"What have I done now?" Archie strode into the room, closed the door behind him and took a seat next to his wife.

"You never take me seriously … but at least the police do." Eliza waved the letter at him. "Look, it's from one of the inspectors in Oxford." She held it out for him to read.

Archie gave the letter a cursory glance. "I'm sure they'd work it out for themselves a lot quicker if they didn't have to respond to everyone writing in with theories of their own."

"Can you see what I have to put up with?" Eliza said to Connie. "Despite the fact the letter says my information was particularly helpful, I never get an ounce of credit around here."

Connie said nothing as her eyes darted between husband and wife.

"Now look what you've done," Eliza said to her husband. "You've made Connie lose her tongue. You need to start being nice to me or she'll go off you."

Archie laughed and took his wife's hand. "I'm always nice to you, in fact, I'm the epitome of niceness. So nice in fact, I came to ask if you'd like me to show you the surgery and your dispensary."

Eliza smiled before studying Archie, her eyes narrowing. "Wait a moment, I'll bet Iris hasn't done any unpacking in there, has she? Is that why you want to show me?"

"If you remember, you told her not to touch anything because you wanted to do it yourself." He turned to Connie. "Sometimes I can't win. I bet the old doctor didn't let his wife help out, did he?"

"No, bless him, he did it all himself. Before she died, his wife kept the surgery clean, but she couldn't do anything with medicines. Not like Eliza, she's so clever."

Eliza's cheeks flushed. "Hasn't there been a doctor here since he died?"

"We've had locums for the last few months, but only two days a week. I imagine you'll be busy once you open."

"Well, I'm not doing anything tonight," Eliza said. "I've done more than enough for one day. We'll set to first thing tomorrow morning and put a sign in the post office window to tell everyone we're opening on Thursday."

CHAPTER TWO

The following morning, breakfast was a hurried affair, and as soon as they had finished their cups of tea, Eliza and Archie left the dining table and went straight to the surgery.

"At least we won't get wet on the way to work," Archie said. "Whoever designed the building was very thoughtful linking the surgery to the house."

"It used to be two houses," Eliza said, "but around the time I left for London the doctor in charge bought the house that's now the surgery and joined the two together. I remember it caused quite a stir at the time. The surgery was only a small house, but it was one less for the villagers to live in. I can't say I'm sorry, can you imagine living and working in the one house?"

"I can't imagine *you* living in half the house, although most people would manage perfectly well," Archie said. "You'll have to show me later where your old house is. Did your father like big houses even in those days?"

Eliza's thoughts drifted back to the memory of her

childhood home. "It's not as big as the one he has now, but I'll admit it's probably the biggest house in the village." She stood in the wood-panelled hallway of the surgery, surveying the doors leading off to the right. "I'm sure we'll be fine though. After all, there's only the two of us now."

"I'm sure Henry will visit his old ma and pa soon enough. His allowance won't stretch until September."

Eliza smiled at the mention of her son. "The term finishes at the end of this week. Why he couldn't come straight here, I don't know."

"I'm sure London is much more exciting to an eighteen-year-old than an out-of-the-way village."

"He's just had a whole term in Cambridge, he should want to come here for a rest."

"And I'm sure he will. As soon as we've moved in and there's no chance he'll be called upon to help us unpack."

Eliza nodded. "You're right, but I worry why he doesn't want to spend any time with us. I suppose there's a reason he's taking after you rather than his grandfather. Managing all those factories would kill him."

"Studying medicine isn't an easy option." Archie gave Eliza a playful scowl. "Despite what people might say, it's not only a matter of cutting people open any more. It's a responsible job."

"And clearly too responsible for women to do."

Archie shook his head as Eliza walked into the room nearest the front door.

"Are you going to unpack the medicines while I take a look through the records the old doctor left?"

"I will if we have the space." Eliza stood in the middle of the room and glanced around. It was a modest room by her standards, maybe fifteen feet long by twelve feet wide, fitted with a range of mahogany cupboards and drawers neatly arranged behind a long, matching counter along the back wall. Half a dozen wooden chairs lined the wall opposite the door while the sun illuminated the room as it shone through a large sash window to the front.

"There'll be plenty of room. We didn't bring that many medicines with us."

Eliza frowned. "We didn't, but we acquired a lot of stock when we bought the surgery and so there might not be much extra room. Now, be off with you while I get on. I'd like to get everything unpacked before luncheon."

Once she was alone, she walked to the cupboards and pulled open those nearest to her. All she had to do was unload the crates and boxes standing in the middle of the room into the available space. *Where do I start?* Thank goodness Iris had arrived several days earlier. She'd cleaned and polished all the surfaces and existing bottles and made sure they were in alphabetical order. It shouldn't be difficult.

With homes found for the books and most of the equipment, Eliza lifted the final boxes onto the counter. There was a lovely display shelf behind the cabinet for her ornamental coloured glass jars and she polished them carefully before arranging them in symmetrical rows. Satisfied with her work, she turned her attention to the medicines. Another twenty minutes and she'd be finished.

She opened the first box but paused as she noticed the contents. She hadn't packed them like that. When they left London, she'd wedged the bottles in tight to stop them moving, but now there were gaps. She lifted them onto the counter and lined them up. Was she imagining it? She emptied the remaining boxes, noticing nothing else unusual, before returning to double-check the empty crates. Some bottles were missing. She did a full turn, studying each shelf as she did. *No, they're not here.*

She wandered out into the hall and down towards the surgery at the far end. "Darling, are you there?"

Archie looked up from his reading. "Did you say something?"

"Have you taken anything from the crates in the front room?" Her eyes rested on several empty boxes on the examination table. "Or is there anything of mine in here that hasn't been unpacked yet? What about these?"

Archie looked over to the boxes. "No, I think they're empty. Iris helped me put all my stuff away earlier and I've not touched anything in the dispensary. What have you lost?"

"I'm not sure, but I'm worried a couple of bottles have disappeared."

Archie stood up and the two of them walked back to the dispensary. "What are you missing?"

Eliza sighed. "That's what's annoying me. I can't be sure. I think one is codeine tablets, but I can't remember what else we had in London."

The doctor studied the collection of bottles in front of him. "All the usual things are here, and so I imagine it's something we don't use very often. I'm sure they'll turn up. Why don't you ask Iris when we go back to the house? She may have unpacked some of your things for you before realising you wanted to do it yourself."

"Yes, I'm sure you're right. Let me get this lot locked away and I'll go and ask her."

. . .

Iris was in the kitchen when Eliza found her.

"No, I've not been in the dispensary, madam. I pointed the removals men in the right direction and came back into the house to supervise here."

"How strange. I'm sure we packed everything. I checked the old house after they had taken the boxes and there was nothing left. They must be here somewhere. Never mind. Let's get something to eat and I'll carry on looking later."

With luncheon over, Eliza stood up to leave the table as there was a knock on the front door. A moment later, Iris showed Connie in.

"You're late. Are you still keeping London time?" Connie said.

Eliza glanced at the grandfather clock by the door. "We were so busy unpacking I didn't notice the time. What can I do for you?"

"It's such a lovely day, I thought we could go for a walk around the village. It might not look like it, but a lot's changed since you left and there are plenty of new people for me to introduce you to."

Eliza hesitated. "I'm not sure..."

"If you want, we could walk over to your old house. It's not changed much but I thought you might like to see it." Connie's eyes pleaded with Eliza. "I've been so looking forward to showing you off around the village."

Eliza held up her hands. "How can I refuse? I was going to stay in and look for a couple of bottles that have gone missing from the dispensary, but where's the fun in that? I'll look for them later. I don't suppose anything's going to happen to them and you're right. It would be a shame to miss the weather. Besides, I need to put up a notice in the post office about the surgery opening. Shall we go there first?"

Connie held the door open for Eliza as they left the post office. "Are you sure you'll be ready to open by Thursday? It only gives you another day to sort yourselves out."

"We'll be fine. The poor people around here haven't had access to a doctor all week, and if we leave it until next week we'll be inundated. No, let's get a couple of days under our belts and then we can take some time off at the weekend." Eliza paused and surveyed the neatly kept bowling green situated on the inside of the bend at the top end of the village green. "You've got a new pavilion."

"And not before time either. The old one was about to fall down, but they reached their savings target at the end of last summer and the rebuilding finished a couple of weeks ago."

The sun bounced off the white wooden walls causing Eliza to shade her eyes with a hand. "Good for them. I wonder if Archie would enjoy bowling. I'll suggest he gets involved once he's settled in. It'll do him good. Now, where shall we go first?"

"How about we take the footpath across the village green, behind the pavilion and visit your old house, then we can walk back around the road and I'll show you some of the newer houses?"

Eliza nodded. "Lead the way then."

The sun ducked in and out from behind the clouds as they walked along the footpath.

"It'll seem strange seeing the house again after all these

years," Eliza said. "Did the new people you were telling me about arrive in the spring?"

"They did, but they might as well not have bothered. Nobody's seen hide nor hair of them since they arrived, not even the housekeeper. Rumour has it they're from London and we think they travel back there on a regular basis."

"Perhaps they haven't taken to village life. I don't suppose it's for everyone."

"If you ask me, they haven't given it a chance."

"Don't you know anything about them?"

Connie shook her head. "Not much. The current view is there are at least four children, three girls and a boy, but to be honest, I suspect that's only Mrs Petty's guesswork. If there's something she doesn't know, she'll make it up."

Eliza laughed. "The village gossip is she?"

"You could say that."

"So why are we going there now? Are you sure it's for my benefit or is it just an excuse for you to be nosy?"

Connie's cheeks coloured and the corners of her mouth turned upwards. "Me, nosy? I don't know what you mean."

As they approached the far side of the village green, Eliza spotted two women leaving one of the larger houses. The younger of the two would have been tall and elegant had it not been for the pronounced stoop as she walked. She was pushing the older woman in a wheelchair.

"Who's this coming towards us?" Eliza asked.

Connie gave her a sideways glance. "Don't you recognise her? It's Judith Wilson, Judith Roberts as was. You must remember her. From school?"

Eliza's brow creased. "Who did she marry then? Not Joseph Wilson?"

"Yes, I'm sure I told you."

"I'm sure you didn't. I'd remember something like that. What's happened to her? Is she ill?"

"You're about to find out, but let me tell you, the woman in the wheelchair is Mr Wilson's mother, now known as Mrs Milwood after her second marriage. I'll introduce you."

Within seconds the ladies came together.

"Judith, how nice to see you, and you too, Mrs Milwood." Connie put on her best smile but a seething glare from Mrs Milwood caused it to freeze on her lips.

"Aren't you going to introduce me to your friend? You wouldn't make a very fine hostess."

"Y-Yes, of course. Don't you remember her? This is Mrs Eliza Thomson, the new doctor's wife … Eliza Bell as was."

"Eliza?" Judith's face broke into a smile. "How lovely!"

"So you're back, are you?" Mrs Milwood interrupted. "You take note, Judith, everyone comes back in the end. Taking my son back to London won't work. You can go on your own if you want to, nobody will miss you."

Judith closed her eyes and clenched the handles of the wheelchair until her knuckles turned white, while Mrs Milwood turned her attention to Eliza.

"What are you staring at? That fancy education didn't get you far, did it? I don't know why they even bother educating women."

"What a terrible attitude." Eliza's eyes widened.

"Nonsense. How much of your father's money did you waste? And now you're back, no better than the rest of us. You don't need an education to learn how to keep a house."

"She's not just keeping house, she'll be working in the dispensary…" Connie said.

"Working in the dispensary?" For a moment Eliza thought Mrs Milwood would step out of the wheelchair and accost her. "Well, don't expect to do anything for me. I've been waiting for the new doctor to arrive for weeks and I don't expect him to pass half his work to someone with ideas above her station. Come on, Judith, we haven't got all day; I need my walk."

Judith thrust the wheelchair forward, her expression mortified. "I'm sorry; will you excuse us?"

Eliza nodded. "Yes, of course. Call in any time ... when you get a minute."

Judith said nothing but pushed the chair past them, her frame once again slouched over the old woman.

"What on earth happened to Judith?" Eliza asked when they were alone. "She used to be such fun."

"Three years of living with Mrs Milwood. Nobody knows how she manages, poor thing. Judith's told me they had a good life in London until Mrs Milwood's second husband died, leaving her a wealthy woman. That was when they were summoned back to Moreton and Mrs Milwood now expects Judith and Mr Wilson to take care of her. She's threatened to disinherit them if they don't."

"Is Mrs Milwood always so nasty?"

Connie grimaced. "You're fortunate she took an immediate dislike to you. She'd have interrogated you for hours otherwise while she found a reason to criticise you."

Eliza put a hand to her heart. "Thank goodness for that. At least my education wasn't a waste of time if it cut short that exchange. Come on, let's keep going. Hopefully Judith will call in to the surgery and we can have a proper talk with her then."

It was another ten minutes before Eliza and Connie reached the front gates of Oak House, an impressive three-storey mansion at the far end of an exclusive cul-de-sac. Eliza peered through the gates of her former home and turned to Connie. "There it is, looking as grand as ever. I wish Father hadn't sold it."

"It wasn't his fault."

"No." For the first time in years, Eliza let her mind drift back to her childhood and the dreadful days following her mother's death.

Connie put a hand on her arm. "I shouldn't have brought you. It was a long time ago and I thought…"

Eliza blinked and took a deep breath, pulling herself up to her full height. "No, you were right to bring me. I had to come sooner or later and it was better to get it out of the way. Come on, if we're going to walk the long way round we'd better get a move on. Just be ready to throw yourself into a bush if we spot Judith and Mrs Milwood coming the other way. I've no appetite for talking to that woman ever again."

CHAPTER THREE

Eliza reached for the nearest chair and hauled herself back to her feet, flicking the dust from her skirt as she did.

"What on earth are you doing?" Archie wandered into the dispensary where Iris was also pushing herself to her feet.

"Looking for those bottles. I wondered if they'd rolled under the cupboards, but we can't find them anywhere. We've gone back through all the boxes but they've disappeared."

"Are you sure you packed them? Could we have left them in London?"

"I hope not." Eliza's brow furrowed. "No, the only place they would have been in the old house was the study, and I checked the room once the boxes had gone. There was nothing left."

"Well, they must be here somewhere, then. I'm sure they'll turn up."

Eliza sighed and studied the clock. "I suppose so. Come on, we'd better go through to the dining room. Cook will be wondering where we are."

Archie held the door open as the ladies filed past him.

"Don't worry about the bottles. Why don't you take yourself out again this afternoon instead? Once we open tomorrow, you'll be too busy to go very far. You said yourself you didn't see everything you wanted to yesterday, and I'm sure Connie will be glad to escort you again."

With luncheon over and Archie once again in his surgery, Eliza reached for her hat and a pale blue summer coat before making her way next door.

"Eliza!" Connie's smile lit up her face. "How marvellous of you to call. Come in, come in; please excuse the house." Connie ushered Eliza into her small living room before she rushed to remove her plate and cutlery from the table in the far corner. Seconds later, judging by the noise that came from the scullery, Eliza guessed she'd thrown them into the sink.

"Sorry about that," Connie said as she returned to the room. "I'm running late."

"That's not like you, what have you been doing?"

Without pausing for breath, Connie hurried to the two chairs in front of the fireplace to shake the cushions. "I decided to tidy the big cupboard upstairs, and it took me longer than I thought. Why don't you take a seat while I go and wash up? It won't take me a minute."

As Connie disappeared, Eliza studied the compact living room. Alongside the table and chairs stood a wooden dresser, while the armchairs by the fire took up most of the front portion of the room. She perched on one of the seats and waited for Connie to reappear. "I didn't call to judge the place."

"Even so, I have my pride. The house might only be small, but I like it to be well presented."

"And very nice it is too."

Connie's cheeks reddened. "I'm glad you like it and at least it's mine. Mr Appleton made sure I was provided for before he died."

Eliza stood up and took hold of Connie by the shoulders. "Connie, stop. Your house is lovely and you're very fortunate, but I only called to ask if you wanted to take a walk."

"A walk, are you sure?"

"Of course I'm sure, why wouldn't I be?"

Connie exhaled and let her shoulders relax. "I'd love to. I wanted to ask you the same question, but I thought you might have seen enough of me for one week."

Eliza rolled her eyes. "Don't be silly, you'll tire of me before I stop calling. You're the only one I know around here."

Connie's face broke into a smile. "Splendid, let me get my coat."

"You can introduce me to a few more people as we go, as long as no one else around here is like Mrs Milwood."

"No, she's the worst," Connie said. "We'd better keep an eye open for her though, in case Judith's taken her for a walk."

Once Connie had fixed her hat and coat, the two of them turned left out of the house, past the surgery, towards to the shop.

"Who's the vicar at the church nowadays? I take it the old reverend has long gone?"

"Reverend Lamb his name is. He's been here at least ten years now. Another one who moved from London to get away from all the noise."

"Is he married?"

Connie shook her head. "No. He's a nice enough man, but never settled down with anyone. He lives in the vicarage on his own but he has a cook and a housekeeper who come in daily. Mr Hewitt's churchwarden now and he spends most of his days round there."

"Mr Hewitt who used to run the Sunday school?"

"That's him. He still keeps an eye on the Sunday school, in fact he keeps an eye on pretty well everything involving the church." Connie gave a chuckle. "Some folks reckon he even checks over the vicar's sermon before he preaches on a Sunday."

Eliza gazed up at the medieval church as they approached it. "If he's anything like he used to be, that wouldn't surprise me. Perhaps I'll leave meeting him until I go to church. Shall we keep walking?"

Beyond the church, the road curved round to head back down the other side of the village. A row of benches lined the inside of the bend overlooking the bowling green, but they were empty at this time of day.

"I look forward to sitting there in the summer watching the bowls," Eliza said.

"It is a lovely spot but I don't enjoy coming on my own. Somehow it doesn't seem right."

"Well, you won't be on your own this year, although who's that? There's someone on their own over there." Eliza nodded to a bench opposite the police station. "It looks like Judith."

"I think you're right, although it's most unusual for her to be on her own at this time of the afternoon."

Eliza scanned the surroundings. "There's no chance of Mrs Milwood being anywhere close by, is there?"

"I doubt it, unless Judith's taken her somewhere and left her."

Eliza laughed. "I can't imagine why she'd do that."

The sound of laughter caused Judith to turn towards them and her face instantly lit up as she waved at them.

"Connie, Eliza, over here. Come and sit with me."

"You look cheerful," Connie said as they sat down. "What have you done with Mrs Milwood?"

Judith smiled. "She was complaining of feeling unwell and so I put her to bed and took the opportunity to spend some time by myself."

"That was a stroke of luck. After yesterday, we'd hoped we might bump into you. Mrs Milwood was more cantankerous than ever. Were you all right after you left us?"

Judith grimaced. "Oh, she was in a terrible mood, but I'm used to it by now. Fortunately, when she's in her wheelchair her words project forwards and not backwards, and given she can't see me, I switch off and leave her to it."

Connie's sniggering brought the smile back to Judith's lips.

"You're a bad influence." Judith tapped Connie's hand.

"Do you want me to ask Dr Thomson to call on her?" Eliza said.

"Oh gracious, no, she'll be fine. I'm sure you noticed she's an expert at complaining. She was only a little sickly before luncheon but she has to make sure she gets every ounce of sympathy. By the time I get home, she'll be up and poking her nose into everyone else's business again."

"Is she always as bad as she was yesterday?" Eliza asked.

Judith scowled. "I can only apologise. Unfortunately for

you, she'd argued with Flora, my daughter, shortly before we left the house, and you got the end of it."

"You have a daughter?" Eliza said. "How old is she?"

"Seventeen, although she wishes she were older. She wants to go to university in London but her grandmother is dead set against it. You happened to catch her at the wrong time."

"What about you and Mr Wilson? Are you happy for her to go?" Eliza asked.

Judith shrugged her shoulders. "Our opinions don't make any difference, Mother's the one with the money and so she'll make sure she has the final say."

"How awful. Why's she so against it?"

"Because she's a miserable old woman!" Judith's voice boomed across the bowling green and they all burst into laughter. "Oh, it felt good to say that."

"Well, you should say it more often. If you come to the surgery, you can say things like that whenever you like. Consider it a form of therapy."

"I may take you up on that!"

"I once heard Mrs Milwood say the best way for a woman to make a good life for herself is to find a wealthy husband," Connie said. "Maybe you should find her another one and send her on her way."

Judith sighed. "Wouldn't that be nice? The only problem is, nobody would want her."

"They may not want her, but many would be happy to take her if she had her money with her. You should advertise." Connie raised an eyebrow.

"A notice in the post office window?" Judith said. "What

would we write? *Grouchy old woman free to a good home, comes with a substantial inheritance.*"

Connie and Judith fell into each other as they laughed.

"You are mean." Eliza tried to keep her face straight but failed. "Well, at least we've cheered you up ... oh my goodness!" She put a hand to her chest and visibly jumped as the church bells struck three. "Those bells will be the death of me. There must be quieter places to sit."

Judith bit her lip as she tried to be serious. "They are loud when you sit here, but I'm sure you'll get used to them. They're not so bad when you're indoors with the windows shut. Anyway, they're telling me it's time I was going." The joy that had brightened Judith's face disappeared. "I've been sat here for over an hour and no doubt she'll be waiting with some instructions when I get back."

"Why don't you walk the long way around with us?" Eliza said. "I'm sure she won't miss you for an extra five or ten minutes."

Judith glanced at the church clock and accepted the invitation without hesitation.

"You're welcome to stay for afternoon tea," Eliza said as they began walking. "After what Mrs Milwood said to you yesterday, she needs to realise how much she'd miss you if you did leave."

Judith's eyes flicked between Eliza and Connie as the smile returned. "I will as well ... but not today. She was poorly when I left and so I suppose I'd better go and see how she is. Maybe one day next week?"

. . .

With afternoon tea over and Connie heading home, Eliza returned to the dispensary and cast her eyes around the room. For a small rural practice, it looked well equipped, and she smiled at the thought that by this time tomorrow they would have done their first day.

"What are you smiling at?" Archie said as he joined her.

"I'm thinking how smart the place looks. Is the surgery ready for tomorrow?"

"As ready as it needs to be. I left Iris doing a final clean and I'll read through the old patient notes when each of them come to see me. No point reading them all yet."

"I suppose this calls for a celebration. Would you like a glass of sherry before dinner?"

"What a marvellous idea. Give me another ten minutes and I'll join you in the drawing room."

With Iris busy, Eliza helped herself to a couple of glasses of sherry and placed one on each of the side tables next to the fire before taking a seat on the settee overlooking the garden. Connie was right. This was a nice room with the sun shining in and it was especially nice having the river running across the bottom of the garden.

As soon as he arrived, Archie raised a toast. "To Moreton-on-Thames. May we always be happy here."

"Moreton-on-Thames," Eliza repeated as she clinked her glass against her husband's.

"You need to take me for a walk around the village on Sunday so I can see where everyone lives," Archie said. "I can't be turning up for house visits late because I can't find where I'm going."

Eliza chuckled. "The village isn't very big, I'm sure you'll work it out soon enough." She took a sip of her sherry but groaned when there was a knock on the front door. "Who on earth can this be at this time of day? Surely they could have waited until tomorrow?"

Seconds later, Iris knocked on the door and showed Mr Wilson in. "Mr Wilson's here for you, Dr Thomson."

Eliza swivelled in her seat as Archie stood up and extended his hand to the man in front of him.

"Mr Wilson, what can I do for you?" Archie asked.

"You must come quickly, Doctor. It's my mother, Mrs Milwood. She's dead."

CHAPTER FOUR

E liza sprang from her chair, spilling some of her sherry onto the floor.

"Oh my goodness." Eliza caught her breath. "Judith said she was ill, but thought she'd be well again by the time she got home. Are you sure she's not just sleeping?"

Mr Wilson's eyes were wide. "She's very pale and cold to the touch. We think she's been dead for a while."

Archie headed for the door. "Let me get my bag and you can show me the way."

"I'll come with you and sit with Judith," Eliza said. "She must be in a state of shock."

"She is rather upset," Mr Wilson said. "She was the one who found her. I've only just got home from work."

Archie nodded his consent to Eliza. "Very well, but be quick with your hat and coat."

Within minutes the three of them were heading across the village green and by the time they arrived at the house, Eliza was exhausted.

"Did you have to walk so fast? I'm not used to it."

Her complaint remained unanswered as the church bells struck five o'clock.

"Come on in." Mr Wilson pushed open the front door. "Judith must be with Mother, it's this way."

Mr Wilson led them to a room at the back of the house on the ground floor. The curtains had been drawn and the only light was from a single candle on the bedside cabinet. In the darkness it took a moment for Eliza to spot Judith sitting at the foot of the bed. She stood up as they entered.

"Dr Thomson, Eliza, thank you for coming." She took Eliza's hands. "I didn't know what to do. After I left you, I came straight home but when Mother didn't call for me, I asked Cook to make me a cup of tea. I took it in the drawing room and didn't come in here until I'd finished it. When I did I found her lying here, just as she is now."

Eliza put an arm around Judith's shoulders while Archie walked to the bedside and felt for a pulse.

"Would you mind putting the lights on?" he asked. "I need to see what I'm doing."

With the room illuminated, Eliza suspected he would find no sign of life.

"I'm sorry," he said, after a brief examination of the body. "You're right. I would say she's been dead for several hours."

"It must have been sometime after half past one," Judith said. "That was when I left for my walk; I was back about two hours later, but as I said, I didn't come in here until after I'd had a cup of tea."

"She told me once that one of the visiting doctors had suggested she had a bad heart," Mr Wilson said. "Could that be what did it?"

"It's a possibility but I'll need to arrange a post-mortem to confirm the cause of death," Archie said.

Eliza studied the body, her brow furrowed.

"Are you sure that's necessary?" Mr Wilson said. "She was an elderly woman with a weak heart. Do you need to waste time on a post-mortem?"

"Just procedure, nothing to be worried about."

"There seems to be a strange smell." Eliza spoke to herself, but noticed Judith tense as she spoke. "You mentioned Mrs Milwood was feeling sickly, was she actually sick?"

Judith's cheeks coloured. "Only a little."

"But there's no sign of it and you said you haven't touched the body."

"No, I didn't." Judith shook her head vigorously. "But ... well, it soiled the bedcover, and I wanted to change it before the doctor arrived. It was only the top cover, which is why I didn't touch the body."

"Do you have the soiled covers to hand, Mrs Wilson?" Archie asked. "A sample would be useful."

Judith lowered her gaze. "No, I'm afraid I don't. I put them straight into some water and rinsed them out when Joseph came for you."

Archie's shoulders sagged as he let out a deep breath. "That's unfortunate, never mind."

"What's that over there?" Eliza pointed to a mark on the rug next to the bed and moved to take a closer look. "Can you use this as a sample?"

Judith shivered as Archie examined the rug. "What must you think of me not tidying up properly?"

"We don't think anything of it," Eliza said. "You had other concerns."

31

"Yes, of course, thank you." Judith nodded and waited for Archie to collect the sample. "If you have everything you need, I'll show you out."

"Before we go, I need to take a couple of other samples and arrange the body for collection," Archie said. "We can't leave her like this until the morning. Eliza, why don't you take Mr and Mrs Wilson into one of the other rooms and wait for me?"

Eliza guided Judith from the room. "Shall we go to the drawing room?"

Judith nodded. "I feel so awful that we were laughing about her this afternoon. It's as if God's punishing me."

"Don't be silly, these things happen and she was elderly." Eliza hesitated and turned to see Mr Wilson still in the bedroom. "This may sound like a strange question, but do you have a medicine cabinet?"

"Yes, of course. It's in the kitchen, why?"

"Mr Wilson mentioned his mother had a weak heart and I wondered if the doctor who saw her prescribed any medication. Could I take a look in the cabinet now? It may help with the post-mortem."

Judith hesitated. "I don't remember seeing anything, but you can look if you like."

Eliza followed Judith into a good-sized, brightly lit kitchen where a short woman wearing a floral pinny and white elasticated cap stood alongside a cooking range on the far side of the room. The smell of onions and herbs from the pan she was stirring filled the room.

"Are you nearly ready to eat?" Cook asked Judith. "This dinner will be ruined if you leave it much longer."

Judith let out a deep sigh. "Mrs Harris, I'm sorry to say

that sometime this afternoon, Mrs Milwood was taken from us. The doctor's with her now."

The cook's brow creased as her rosy cheeks paled. "Taken? You mean dead?"

"Yes, unfortunately, that is what I mean. Please don't be distressed; we know how much you cared for her."

Mrs Harris staggered to the nearest chair. "Well I never, who'd have thought...? Do you know what did it?"

"No, not yet but we wanted a quick look in the medicine cabinet if you don't mind. Mrs Thomson here is the wife of the new doctor and she'd like to know if Mother was taking any medicines for her heart."

"Not that I know of, although I wouldn't have been the one to give them to her. Help yourself." Mrs Harris got back to her feet. "I'll take the stew off the heat and give myself five minutes. You've given me quite a stir."

"Yes, you take your time. We'll be a little while yet." Judith moved towards a cabinet situated on the wall next to the door. "Here you are, Eliza."

"Is this it?" Eliza studied the empty shelves. "Some tonic wine, a herbal medicine and a few codeine tablets."

Judith nodded. "The tablets were for her joints. She had problems with them being painful and stiff; that's why I always pushed her out in the wheelchair."

"What about the other two, were they for her joints as well?"

"I'm not sure; she often refused to tell me what things were for. I'd take her to the surgery, but she always saw the doctor alone. She never told me anything I didn't need to know."

Eliza examined the bottles. "They don't look as if they were for her joints. Do you know if she took either today?"

"Now you're asking ... I don't remember, if I'm being honest."

Eliza paused and scanned the rest of the kitchen. "Are you sure there's nowhere else in the house she might have kept her medicines?"

"Well, no. She couldn't manage the stairs on her own and so we kept everything down here for her."

"Here you are," Mr Wilson interrupted. "I thought you'd got lost. Is there a problem?"

"I'm sure there isn't," Eliza said, "but when you said your mother had a weak heart, I wondered if the doctor had prescribed her any medicine for it. It doesn't look like there's anything relevant in here, but Dr Thomson will have her patient notes so he can look back at them once we get home."

Judith shuddered. "Shall we wait for him in the drawing room? I don't know about you, but I could do with a brandy. Do you mind?"

"My dear, of course not. You've both had a terrible shock. Please don't mind me, I'm sure Archie won't be long."

Once they were in the drawing room, Mr Wilson poured himself and his wife a drink.

"Will you join us, Mrs Thomson?"

"No, thank you. A small glass of sherry's about my limit, and I have one waiting for me at home."

Mr Wilson handed Judith a brandy. "What an evening."

"It's a good job it happened today." Judith's hands trembled as she clutched the glass. "If it had been last week, there wouldn't have been a doctor to call on."

"Don't worry about that now. Dr Thomson's here and he'll sort everything out."

As the silence lingered Eliza glanced around the room and admired the large windows that overlooked the garden. "I know it's too early to say for certain, but once the formalities are out of the way, are you likely to stay here or move back to London?"

Mr Wilson shrugged. "I imagine it will take us a while to wrap everything up here. Then we'll see. We need to tell the children first. As soon as Judith told me I came for your husband. Nobody else knows."

"How many children do you have?"

Judith gave a faint smile. "Three, two boys and a girl."

"That's nice. I only have the one son, Henry. He's not moved with us though; he's in his first year at Cambridge. Studying medicine like his father." Eliza tried to keep the pride from her voice. "Are your children still at home?"

Mr Wilson's face hardened. "Two of them are, Flora and our youngest son Frank. Our eldest, Sam, moved out several weeks ago."

Eliza noticed the sadness in Judith's eyes. "Did he go to London?"

Mr Wilson replied. "No, only to Over Moreton. He wouldn't tell us why, but apparently he'd rather rent a room in a lodging house than stay here with us. Poor Judith hasn't seen him since, have you, dear?"

Judith shook her head as a tear ran down her cheek. "He didn't say a word. Just left for work as usual one morning and didn't come back. At least Joseph still sees him at the workshop, but with me being stuck here with Mother..."

"We work together in Over Moreton," Mr Wilson

explained, as a puzzled expression crossed Eliza's face. "At Royal & Sons."

Eliza raised an eyebrow. "Royal & Sons?"

"They make components for railway tracks. I'm an accountant and Sam's a clerk."

"Yes, I'm aware of it," Eliza said. "It's where my father started before he moved to London."

"Of course it is." Mr Wilson's stance stiffened and Eliza bit down on her lip as the silence in the room grew. She'd heard that Mr Royal hadn't been happy when her father had left to set up his own competing company. He'd mentioned once how angry old Mr Royal had been and even now, nearly thirty years later, it looked as if it hadn't been forgotten.

"Of course, it was a long time ago..." Eliza hesitated, but a smile brightened her face when there was a knock on the door and Archie popped his head into the room.

"May I come in?"

"Please do." Mr Wilson walked to the door and held it open.

"I've laid her out so the body can be moved tomorrow. I'll let you know the arrangements for the post-mortem."

"Thank you, Doctor. Can I offer you a brandy?"

Eliza gave a slight shake of her head.

"Thank you for the offer, but no. Please accept our condolences but we must be going. I'll call again tomorrow. Good evening."

The evening was still light as Eliza and Archie left the Wilsons' and headed home across the village green.

"Do you think the death was down to natural causes?" Eliza asked once they were well away from the houses.

"Why shouldn't it be?"

36

"Oh, I don't know. Something about the bedroom didn't feel right."

Archie gave his wife a sideways glance. "You read about too many murders in the newspapers. Can't you see a perfectly normal death for what it is?"

Eliza sighed. "Perhaps you're right, but I can't help having my suspicions. Both Judith and Mr Wilson looked uncomfortable whenever I asked them a question ... and why would Judith change the cover on the bed and wash the soiled one before they came for you? If I'd found a dead body, doing the laundry wouldn't be top of my priorities."

"So you think Mrs Wilson murdered her mother-in-law?"

Eliza's eyes flashed open. "No, not at all, I'm just saying it seems strange. I also wondered about Mr Wilson's claim that his mother had problems with her heart. There was no sign of any heart medicines in the house, and did you notice the way she was lying on the bed?"

Archie's brow creased as he turned to face her. "There was nothing to notice, she was lying flat on her back."

"Exactly. I know that having a weak heart can cover a multitude of problems, but most commonly it would mean the heart wasn't pumping enough blood around the body. If that was the case, wouldn't she have slept propped up on pillows?"

"If heart failure had only recently been diagnosed, the symptoms would be mild, and she had no swelling in her legs. You're thinking of someone with an advanced stage of the disease."

"Well, why was Mr Wilson so keen to make the point?"

"Eliza, you're reading too much into all of this. The man has just lost his mother; I expect he was guessing at the possible cause. Once we've eaten, I'll read her notes and find out what the visiting doctor said."

They walked the rest of the journey in silence until they reached the gate leading to their front door.

"After you." Archie swung the gate open to let Eliza through and as he did, there was the sound of clinking on the garden path. A second later, a bottle rolled on the path in front of them; Eliza bent down to retrieve it.

"It's the bottle of codeine tablets I was looking for." Her eyes were wide as she stared at her husband. "What's it doing in the bushes?"

"There's another one behind the gate." Archie bent down to pick it up. "Chloroform."

"Chloroform, of course, but how on earth did it get there?"

"They must have fallen from the box when the removals men carried them in."

Eliza shook her head. "No. The box they were in hadn't been damaged. Those bottles were taken deliberately. When you request the post-mortem will you ask the doctor to test for codeine and chloroform? In fact, if you took some blood from the body as well as a sample of whatever was on the rug, we could get those analysed straight away. I don't think it's an accident those were the two bottles that disappeared."

Archie rubbed a hand across his face. "I don't know when I'll have time to sort all this out. The surgery opens in the morning and the nearest hospital is almost an hour's drive away in the carriage."

"But we have to. If there is something untoward going on here, we have a duty to find out what. I'll tell you what, why don't we go now and take the samples to the hospital for them to test? I'll come with you and while you're there, you can arrange the post-mortem. We can eat dinner when we get back."

Archie closed his eyes. "So much for a quiet evening. You'd better tell Iris where we're going while I see about hiring a carriage. I'm not driving myself tonight."

CHAPTER FIVE

E liza's feet ached as she walked back from the dispensary to the house. The first morning surgery had been busier than expected, and with her prescriptions prepared, Eliza was ready for luncheon. She picked up the local newspaper from the sideboard and sat at the dining table while she waited for Archie to join her. The news held nothing of interest and she flicked to the births, deaths and marriages hoping she might recognise some names. When she didn't, she folded the paper up and was about to go in search of Archie when there was a knock on the door. Not waiting for Iris, she hurried to answer it.

"A special delivery for Dr Thomson." The assistant postmaster handed her the envelope before backing away down the path.

It must be the results. That was quick. She hurried to the other side of the building and breathed a sigh of relief when the door to the surgery was open. Archie flinched as she burst into the office and thrust the envelope towards him.

"The lab results, I think."

A frown crossed Archie's face as he sat back in his chair. "Already? Can you give me a few minutes to finish off here?"

"I won't bother answering that." She handed him the letter opener. "What does it say?"

Reluctantly, Archie took the envelope and after opening it he studied the letter in silence.

"Well, don't keep it to yourself."

When Archie failed to answer, she moved around the desk and read it for herself.

"Digitalis! So she did have heart failure."

"Not necessarily. I specifically asked the hospital to test for it because of what Mr Wilson said, but even allowing for the unpredictability of digitalis, these levels are too high to be therapeutic. That will be why the lab got back to me so quickly."

"Is there anything else too high?"

Archie read the rest of the letter. "This isn't the full report, only details of the drugs I asked about." Archie pointed to some values halfway down the page. "She had signs of codeine in her system, but they're consistent with her usual daily dose. There's no mention of chloroform."

"Did you check her notes for heart failure?"

"I did, and there's no mention of it."

"So why was Mr Wilson so keen for us to believe she had a heart condition? Do you reckon he knew about the digitalis and wanted us to believe there was a reason for her having taken it?"

Archie sighed as he stood up. "I've no idea, but you know what this means, don't you? We'll need an inquest." He opened the door to let her out. "After luncheon, I need to make a couple of house visits. While I'm out can you put a letter together for the coroner? We need to get it arranged as soon as we can."

As the afternoon rolled on, Eliza couldn't keep her eyes from the clock. What was keeping Archie? She'd miss the last post if he wasn't home soon.

It was almost four o'clock when he arrived home, and Eliza hurried to the door and ushered him into the drawing room.

"Where've you been? The letter's been written for hours, but I wanted to show it to you before I took it to the post office. What do you think? Is it all right?"

Archie read the request for an inquest and nodded as he scrawled his signature across the bottom.

"There. Can I take my coat off now?"

Eliza grinned at him as she scooped up the letter and folded it into an envelope. "You can. You can join me for afternoon tea as well, as long as you ask Iris to make it while I pop to the post office. I won't be long."

She grabbed her handbag and hurried to the door, wasting no time as she donned her hat and coat.

She was relieved to find the post office empty and was back at the surgery in time to hold the door open for Iris as she delivered the tea tray to the drawing room.

"I asked for priority delivery," she said to Archie, as if there had been no pause in the conversation. "They should receive it by the end of the day, and so with a bit of good fortune we should hear back by Saturday at the latest. Have you had any more thoughts about Mrs Milwood?"

"Don't be ridiculous, I've not stopped since nine o'clock this morning. These next few days are going to be hectic. Everyone waited for me rather than seeing the visiting doctor and now I've got this to deal with as well. I thought you said I'd have a quieter life if we moved here."

"I didn't know there'd be a murder two days after we moved, did I? Anyway, I've been thinking. I can't fathom how Mrs Milwood had such high levels of digitalis in her system. Our bottles are still on the shelf where I put them on Tuesday, and Judith said there were no medicines in the house besides those she showed me. Are you going to go over there this afternoon and tell them what you've found? If you are, I'll come with you and check with her again."

Archie paused while he helped himself to a slice of cake. "No, I'm not going over there. I'm afraid to say it, but you might be right about her dying under suspicious circumstances, in which case we could be looking at a murder investigation."

Eliza nodded. "That's what I thought. Should we warn Judith and Mr Wilson? They'll need to delay the funeral, for one thing, and it'll come as a shock if they only find out with everyone else."

Archie puffed up his cheeks. "We can't jump to conclusions ahead of the inquest. You've said yourself, the way both Mr and Mrs Wilson are behaving either could be a suspect. We can't tip them off before we tell the police."

Eliza's eyes widened. "Do you really think it could be one of them?"

Archie shrugged. "That'll be for the police to decide, but

at the moment I can't see anyone else who could have done it."

Eliza sat in silence as she sipped her tea. "We don't know that."

"No, we don't, but it's not for us to find out. I can already see the cogs turning in your head but you have to leave it to the police."

"I helped the police in London ... and it was a good job for you I did."

"I know, but..."

"And the police are particularly bad at investigating poisonings. If it hadn't been for me..."

Archie held up his hands. "Stop. We're not doing anything until after the inquest. Just concentrate on the murders reported in the newspaper like you usually do."

Eliza scowled at her husband before a smile crept to her lips. "You don't usually tell me to do that."

Archie threw his hands in the air. "If it stops you being involved in real murders, then I'll settle for it, and don't go telling Connie anything either. Once the inquest's over you can tell her all you like, but not before. Is that clear?"

"But..."

"No buts. You're in a privileged position as far as the circumstances of the death are concerned and you can't abuse your position."

Eliza's shoulders dropped. "You're right, I won't say a word. I'll just have to hope Connie doesn't call."

"If she does, tell her you're busy, which you are. I need prescriptions making up for the patients I visited this afternoon."

Eliza's shoulders slumped further. Why was it that on her

first day at work, she was annoyed she actually had to do some work? She should be pleased. She glanced over to Archie and sat up straight. She would be ... once she'd helped the police find the killer.

Thankful that their second surgery was less hectic than the first, Eliza found the time the following morning to flick through the local newspaper to see if Mrs Milwood's death was in the obituary column. A smile crossed her face. *There it is.*

'*We regret to announce the death of Mrs Maud Milwood of Moreton-on-Thames. She died peacefully in her sleep on Wednesday, June 13 1900. The funeral date is still to be confirmed, and details will be available from her son, Mr Joseph Wilson, in due course.*'

Eliza raised an eyebrow. *Died peacefully in her sleep. Someone's been rather presumptuous.* She scanned the rest of the page but was interrupted when Iris knocked on the dispensary door.

"There's a letter here for Dr Thomson, special delivery, but his surgery door is shut. Can I leave it with you?"

Eliza hurried to take it from her. "Yes, of course you can. I'll give it to him as soon as he's free."

With a sigh of relief that the final patient didn't need a prescription, Eliza hurried into the surgery.

"This has been delivered. Is it about Mrs Milwood?"

Archie studied the envelope before slicing open the top. "A letter from the coroner. That was quick."

"What's the news?" Eliza's shoulders tensed as she waited

for a response. "How long do I have to keep this whole thing secret?"

Archie scanned the letter. "Not long. He's arranged the inquest for tomorrow. They've written to the police and the family to tell them."

"We'd better get finished here then. If I received a letter like that, I'd be round here in a shot to find out what was going on."

Archie grunted. "Yes, you would, but other folks might not be quite so inquisitive."

Eliza bristled. "Of course they will be. Judith and Mr Wilson will want to know why there's an inquest. It'll look suspicious if they don't."

"It could look suspicious if they do."

"I don't care what you say. We need to take luncheon before the afternoon post arrives, otherwise we'll never get it. Are you ready now?"

Eliza had barely placed her knife and fork back onto her plate when there was a knock on the door.

"What did I tell you?" Eliza's eyes sparkled as she held Archie's gaze. "Who do you think it will be first? My guess is the Wilsons."

Before he could answer there was a knock on the dining room door and Iris popped her head in.

"Mr and Mrs Wilson are here for you, Doctor. I've shown them into the surgery."

"Thank you, Iris, tell them I'll be with them in a moment."

Once they were alone again, Archie stared at the large grin on his wife's face. "You stay here, I'll deal with them."

"But Judith…"

"Judith nothing. I know you. Let me deal with them."

"Humph." Eliza folded her arms and sank back into her chair as Archie left the room. "He wouldn't have even thought of murder if it wasn't for me."

"What did you say?"

Eliza jumped at the sound of her friend's voice. "Connie! I didn't hear you arrive, what are you doing here?"

"Iris saw me walking up the garden path and opened the door before I had a chance to knock. I saw the details of Mrs Milwood's death in the paper and thought you'd have more details. Did you say murder?"

Eliza put a finger to her lips as she hurried to close the door. "Shhh, you're not supposed to know but yes, she was murdered!"

"No!"

"Well, we think so anyway, or at least I do." Her grin grew broader.

"When? How? What makes you think it was murder?"

"It was on Wednesday after we'd met Judith in the village. She got home to find Mrs Milwood dead. Everyone thought it was natural causes, but I wasn't so sure. There were a few things that didn't add up and so Archie requested a post-mortem."

"And they said she was murdered?"

Eliza averted her gaze as she chose her words. "Not directly, but there were high levels of a poisonous drug in her system that we can't account for. They're holding an inquest tomorrow."

Connie's eyes were wide. "An inquest. Is that why Judith and Mr Wilson are here?"

Eliza laughed. "And is that why you're here, because you saw them heading over?"

Connie's cheeks flushed. "Not exactly, although I can't deny I was a little curious. Will you go to the inquest?"

A grin settled on Eliza's face. "Of course I will. Why don't you come too? It's being held in the Black Swan in Over Moreton."

"Why is it being held over there when we have our own public house? Isn't the Golden Eagle good enough?"

"Maybe it's the name. Anything to do with death has to be in the *Black* Swan." Eliza wiggled her fingers towards Connie, who shrieked and moved away.

"You!" Connie chuckled but immediately stopped as Archie came into the room. He glared at them both as if they were naughty schoolgirls.

"Mrs Wilson asked if she could speak to you." His gaze rested on his wife. "Fortunately, I left her in the surgery. Could you please remember she's recently bereaved?"

Eliza raised her eyebrows at Connie. "Why don't you go home and I'll call round once the Wilsons have gone?" With a discreet wink at her friend, she lowered her head and made her way to the surgery.

Judith and Mr Wilson were sitting by Archie's paper-strewn desk, but as soon as Eliza and Archie joined them, Mr Wilson stood up and offered her a seat.

"Please sit down. Dr Thomson and I can go into another room."

Eliza waited for them to leave before placing a hand on Judith's knee. "How are you feeling? Did Archie explain what will happen at the inquest?"

Judith nodded as her eyes filled with tears. "He did, but

48

what do I say? I was the last person to see her alive. Do you think they'll accuse me of her murder?"

"Why should they?"

Judith sobbed into her handkerchief. "Because everyone knew we didn't get along and I was the only one who saw her that day. If it wasn't my fault, who else will they blame?"

When Eliza didn't answer, Judith grabbed her hands. "You've got to believe me, Eliza, I didn't kill her. I can't deny I didn't like her, but I wouldn't have done anything like that. I've never even heard of this digi ... whatever it is. You believe me, don't you?"

Judith's red-rimmed eyes pleaded with Eliza.

"I-I don't know what to believe, but if you say you didn't do it, then yes, I suppose so."

Judith squeezed her hands. "I know how clever you are. Will you find out who did it before the police start asking questions?"

Eliza flinched. "Me? I-I'm not sure ... it should be the police."

"But Connie told me you've done this before, when you were in London. Solved murders, I mean."

"Only once. Most of the time it's from newspaper reports."

"But working out a murder from the newspaper must be even harder than in real life. Please, Eliza, I need your help."

Eliza hesitated as Judith's eyes pleaded with her. "Of course I'll help if I can, but I won't be able to find the murderer before the police get involved. The inquest's tomorrow."

When Judith once again buried her head in her handkerchief, Eliza put an arm around her shoulders. "There,

there, don't worry, I'll help all I can. Let's see what happens tomorrow, shall we? The coroner may come up with a completely different explanation for what happened."

Judith nodded, but the look on her face suggested she didn't believe a word.

CHAPTER SIX

The inquest was due to start at ten o'clock, and Eliza waited outside the surgery with Archie and Connie for the stable boy to bring the carriage round from the back of the house. They hadn't waited long before he arrived.

"Here we are." Archie took the reins and offered his hand to help the ladies into their seats. "Make yourselves comfortable." Climbing onto the driver's seat at the back, he flicked the reins, causing the horses to move forward at a steady trot. Ten minutes later, they pulled up outside the Black Swan.

"This'll be the first time I've been in here." Eliza stared up at the sign hanging outside the front of the building.

"I should hope so," Connie said. "You were only eleven years old when you left Moreton. Your father might have let you do many things, but I'm sure entering a public house wasn't one of them."

Eliza smiled. "You're right ... he'd still raise an eyebrow if he saw me here today."

"I'm sure he wouldn't. Going inside for an inquest is quite different to going in for some liquor."

Before she could reply, a second carriage pulled up behind theirs. "Judith's here." Eliza nodded towards it. "Is that one of her sons with them?"

Connie peered through the window. "I think it's the youngest, Frank. I've not seen him for a few months. It doesn't look like Sam's with them though."

"I never thought to question whether the children would be here," Eliza said. "How old did you say they were?"

Connie put her finger to her chin. "I'm not sure I did, but I've a feeling Judith mentioned Sam would be coming of age later this year and so he must be twenty now. Frank's a couple of years younger so I'd say eighteen or nineteen."

"Old enough I suppose in this day and age."

"Good morning, ladies; Doctor Thomson." Mr Wilson raised his hat to them before turning to help his wife from the carriage. "At least we've got a pleasant day for it. Shall we go in?"

Archie held out his arm to usher the ladies inside while Mr Wilson and his son followed them.

Eliza led Judith to a seat at the front of the room. "How are you feeling?"

Judith's face was white. "I've felt better. I didn't sleep a wink last night worrying about today."

"I'm sure you'll be fine. Just answer the questions honestly."

Judith took a deep breath and nodded. "I will. Thank you."

With the family, police, someone from the local

newspaper and an assortment of other observers assembled, the coroner called the inquest to order.

"Mrs Wilson, would you take the stand, please?"

Eliza squeezed Judith's hand before she made her way to the front of the room.

"Mrs Wilson. I understand you were the last person to see Mrs Milwood alive. Can you tell us exactly what happened on the day of Wednesday the thirteenth of June?"

Judith coughed to clear her throat but her voice was almost inaudible.

"Please speak up, Mrs Wilson. We all need to hear."

Eliza gave her friend a smile and Judith tried again.

"Yes, of course. It was a normal morning to begin with. I took Mother her morning cup of coffee shortly after eight o'clock and she seemed her usual self. She was always groggy first thing and that day was no different."

"Did you help her out of bed?"

"Yes, eventually. I left her to her drink and returned to the room at half past eight. She was in a bad mood because the coffee had been over-sweetened, but I helped her dress and she joined me in the dining room for breakfast."

"And it was just the two of you who took breakfast together? Where were the rest of the family?"

Judith stared at those in the front row as all eyes rested on her. "My husband and youngest son, Frank, had already left for work. They go out at half past seven, before I wake Mother."

"And was that what happened on the day in question?"

"Yes, sir."

"And what about your other children?"

Judith studied the handrail as she paused to answer. "My

eldest son, Samuel, no longer lives with us. He has a room in Over Moreton and I presume he was there. I haven't seen him to ask."

"Your son's grandmother has died, and he hasn't been to see you? Isn't he here?"

Judith shook her head. "We only wrote to tell him the news on Thursday and ... well he's busy. He works, you see."

The coroner made a note on his paper. "And what about your daughter?"

"By the time Mother arrived in the dining room, she'd finished breakfast and gone up to the nursery."

The coroner raised his eyebrows. "The nursery? You still have an infant?"

Judith took a couple of seconds to catch her breath. "No, I'm sorry, she's seventeen now and has a room in the attic she uses as a study. It used to be the nursery and the name's stuck. She's a clever girl..."

The coroner nodded. "And so she didn't see her grandmother that morning?"

"No, sir."

"Tell me what happened after breakfast."

"Well ... yes, nothing much. As usual, I took Mother to the morning room for her to attend to her correspondence and then carried on with some chores."

The coroner stopped her. "You do your own cleaning? Don't you have a maid?"

The pitch of Judith's voice was getting higher. "Usually we do, but our most recent girl left three weeks ago and we haven't got around to replacing her. Mother was seeing to it."

"And in the meantime you were doing the work?"

"Yes, sir. Only the cleaning, though, we still employ a cook."

"And where was this cook on the morning in question?"

"She was in the kitchen, sir. I've asked her since and she said she didn't see Mother that morning. That would be quite usual and I've no reason to doubt her."

The coroner nodded as he added to the notes on the paper in front of him. "What happened next?"

Judith took a deep breath. "Nothing out of the ordinary. Mother and I had morning coffee at eleven o'clock as usual and then shortly afterwards she said she was feeling sickly. After about half an hour I suggested she returned to bed, which she did."

"So what time would that be, half past eleven?"

"Yes, I would say so."

"And then what?"

Judith shrugged. "Well, shortly afterwards, Cook served luncheon for my daughter and I. She wasn't pleased Mother was missing given the effort she'd gone to, but I told her she could have the extra pork chop herself. We finished eating shortly after one o'clock and Flora disappeared back upstairs while I popped in to see Mother. When I realised she was asleep, I decided to take a walk."

"Can you be sure she was sleeping at the time and had not already passed away?"

For the first time Judith smiled. "Yes, sir. Mother had a tendency to snore rather loudly, and so as soon as I put my head around the door I knew she was asleep."

"And so you left her on her own, a woman of advanced years who was feeling unwell, while you went out?"

Judith was silent as she looked at the coroner, tears

filling her eyes. "I thought she'd be fine once she'd had a nap. I expected her to wake up and have me running around after her again. She always kept me busy, so I thought I'd take an hour to myself. I didn't know..." Judith brought her handkerchief to her eyes "...I'd find her ... dead."

Judith's sobs sounded around the room and Mr Wilson jumped up and hurried to his wife's side.

"Sir, please be lenient. My wife's answered all the questions you've posed to her. Can she stand down?"

The coroner nodded. "Yes. I have no further questions for now. Could you escort her back to her seat while I call Dr Thomson?"

Eliza admired Archie as he stood tall on the stand, his broad shoulders setting off the cut of his new suit.

"Dr Thomson, in your initial report you stated that the time of death was likely to be between half past one and two o'clock on Wednesday afternoon." The coroner's voice interrupted Eliza's thoughts. "Can you explain how you can be so precise?"

"Certainly. As you've heard, Mrs Wilson last looked in on Mrs Milwood around one o'clock and her snoring confirmed she was still alive. Mr Wilson then called for me shortly before five o'clock. I remember the time because the church clock struck five as my wife and I arrived at the Wilsons' house. We were immediately shown to the bedroom where Mrs Milwood lay flat on her back with her left arm hanging over the edge of the bed. By the time I examined her, the body had already cooled and parts were starting to stiffen, something that usually takes about three hours. It was also apparent that the arm that had fallen from the bed was beginning to discolour, something that also confirms she had been dead for several hours."

"And so, if what you say is correct, the patient must have died almost immediately after Mrs Wilson left her."

Archie nodded. "It would appear so; however, I would like to suggest that the presence of Mrs Wilson in her mother-in-law's room at one o'clock had no bearing on the victim's death."

There was a low murmuring around the room, causing the coroner to raise his voice to quieten everyone.

"You're referring to the digitalis?" he said once the noise subsided.

"I am indeed. The level of the drug in Mrs Milwood's system was well above the therapeutic levels and was probably toxic. The post-mortem, however, found no evidence that the patient had heart failure, the most likely explanation for the presence of such a drug. Her records also show no evidence she'd been prescribed the drug."

Archie watched Mr Wilson as he shifted in his seat.

"Do go on," the coroner said.

"Well, the fact that Mrs Milwood was physically sick before her death suggests the digitalis was administered either in her food or drink sometime during the previous twelve hours. It's difficult to give an exact time, but I would expect it to be at least two hours prior to her complaints of nausea. Given the condition of her heart and the dosage found in her system, the drug would have needed time to take effect."

The coroner nodded. "So you're suggesting it would have been unnatural for Mrs Milwood to have had such a high dose of digitalis in her system?"

"I am indeed. As I mentioned, Mrs Milwood had never

been prescribed digitalis by her doctor, and after examining the medicine cabinet in the Wilsons' home, I've come to the conclusion someone must have deliberately brought the drug into the house for the purpose of poisoning her."

Archie was forced to stop as the murmuring in the room increased.

"Quiet, please," the coroner shouted above the noise. "This inquest is still in process." He turned back to Archie. "Dr Thomson, did you check with Mr and Mrs Wilson as to the presence of digitalis in any other part of the house?"

"I did, but they said everything was always kept locked in the medicine cabinet."

"So—" the coroner paused to study Archie "–from what you've said, it would appear that the deceased was in fact murdered in her own home and did not die of natural causes."

"That's correct."

The noise level in the room once again increased before the coroner quietened them and Archie continued.

"Given the early symptoms and the nature of the death, I'd suggest the digitalis was administered sometime after one o'clock in the morning when most of the occupants of the house were asleep."

The coroner looked around the room until his eyes settled on Mr Wilson. "Could you tell me what time Mrs Milwood retired for the night?"

"Erm, well ... I'm not sure. She was usually in bed by ten o'clock and I don't remember that evening being any different."

Judith nodded but said nothing.

"Very well then. In that case I'll write up my report this afternoon and send a copy to New Scotland Yard as soon as possible." He looked around the room until his eyes rested on a police officer of average height and above average girth with rosy cheeks and a bushy moustache.

"Sergeant Cooper, there you are. While we wait for a response from the chaps in London, could you pull together a list of suspects for the assigned inspector to interview when he arrives? I'm sure any help you and Constable Jenkins can provide will be most helpful."

Sergeant Cooper studied the tall, thin boy on his left-hand side before nodding.

"Yes, sir. We can do that."

CHAPTER SEVEN

E liza was sitting between Connie and Judith, and shuffled in her seat as the coroner rose and left the room.

"Do you think they believed me?" Judith's eyes were moist as she turned to face her.

"You did very well and Archie's testimony should have helped you. He made it clear that the digitalis could have been given at any time during the twelve hours before you left Mrs Milwood alone. That broadens the list of people who could have given her the medicine."

"But it still suggests someone inside the house did it. With the exception of Mr Hewitt the churchwarden, who called the day before she died, we'd had no visitors for nearly a week. That means..." Mrs Wilson dabbed her eyes with her handkerchief. "That means if it wasn't me, it must have been one of my family."

Eliza hesitated and glanced at Connie. "There may be another explanation ... we just need to make sure we find out the truth."

"Excuse me, ladies."

Eliza looked up as Mr Wilson arrived at the side of his wife.

"If you don't mind, I'd like to take Judith home now. She's had a difficult morning ... not to mention a trying week, she needs to rest."

"Of course." Eliza took hold of Judith's elbow and helped her to her feet. "I'll call with Connie in the next day or two to see how you are."

"And if you could do anything to find the killer..."

"Leave it with us, we'll see what we can find out."

Eliza stood beside Connie and watched as Mr Wilson helped Judith from the room.

"What do you say to that then?" Connie asked once they were alone. "It doesn't look good for them, does it?"

"I'm afraid it doesn't, but there's something not right. It's all too easy. If Judith or Mr Wilson were the murderer, surely they wouldn't have left themselves with no alibi?"

"But they have alibis," Connie said. "Judith was on a bench by the bowling green with us, and Mr Wilson was at work."

Eliza sighed. "They were alibis for when she died, not for when the poison was administered. Archie explained..."

"I know, but they may have hoped nobody would find out. If they were trying to make it look like natural causes, then the best time to have an alibi would be for when she died."

"Yes, you're right, except ... I don't know, something about the timing doesn't add up, but I can't put my finger on it." A frown settled on Eliza's face. "The fact is, according to Archie, someone poisoned her in the early hours of the morning when everyone was in bed, but that gives none of them an alibi.

Even if you wanted people to think it was natural causes, you wouldn't leave yourself open to suspicion like that. Would you?"

Connie shrugged. "Maybe they didn't realise that."

"Possibly ... but if someone was clever enough to know what they were doing, they should have realised that. I don't know. I can't help thinking that someone was trying to make it look like either Mr or Mrs Wilson was the murderer, when in fact they weren't."

Archie walked up behind Eliza and took her elbow. "Are you working on conspiracy theories again?" His smile was tender, but she glared at him causing him to roll his eyes at Connie. "I'm afraid you'll have to put up with this for a few days. Whenever there's a new murder in the newspaper, it's all she can talk about."

Connie's face flushed. "But ... she has a point, don't you think?"

Archie shook his head. "Not you as well."

Eliza pulled her arm from Archie's grasp. "Judith's asked us to help her. She doesn't want the police involved."

"I'm not surprised, she's the prime murder suspect!" Archie retook Eliza's arm and encouraged her towards the door. "Really, you need to stop these games and let the police deal with the investigation. You heard the coroner. He's passing the report to an inspector from New Scotland Yard, but in the meantime Sergeant Cooper's taking charge."

With luncheon over, Eliza slipped on her hat and coat and hurried next door to see Connie.

"I hope you don't mind me calling, my dear, but I can't sit

on my own while Archie's in one of these moods. He never takes me seriously when I'm working through the suspects and I need more information."

"Do you think I can help?" Connie's face lit up with a smile.

"I hope so."

Eliza took off her coat.

"Don't you want to go for a walk while we talk?"

Eliza shook her head. "I need to take notes. I want to try and solve the mystery before the police do. I'll show Archie."

Connie sighed. "Let me put the kettle on then."

With a teapot on the table and her pen and paper in front of her, Eliza listed all those who had come into contact with Mrs Milwood in the twenty-four hours prior to her death.

"So, we have Judith and Mr Wilson, their son Frank and daughter Flora. How are they as a family? Are they happy?"

Connie shrugged. "It's always hard to tell. Judith never looked happy when she was pushing Mrs Milwood around the village, but thinking about it, you rarely saw any other member of the family taking her out. The only time they were all out together was in church and you can't tell much there."

Eliza stared at the teapot as she thought. "No. I wonder if that was because they all disliked her. If they all wanted to be back in London, and she was the only reason they stayed..."

"Or rather her money was the only reason they stayed," Connie said. "Don't forget, Mrs Milwood was a wealthy woman who liked to control the finances rather than let Mr Wilson do it. I would imagine he resented that."

Eliza suddenly sat up straight. "You might be right, but what about a will? If she had that much money, she should have made one."

"I suppose so, but you'll have to ask the family."

"It'll be one of my first questions." Eliza wrote a note across the top of the page. "All right then, now what about the cook? Do you ever speak to her?"

"She's nice enough, but I only say good morning to her in church. She never sits with the family, although I don't suppose you'd expect her to."

"Have you ever spoken to her about the family or picked up any signs that there were problems?"

"I can't say I have."

"Well, this isn't getting us very far." Eliza stood up and paced the room. "What about Mr Hewitt? They said at the inquest he'd visited the house the previous evening."

"They did, but I can't imagine he'd be responsible. He's the churchwarden."

"He may be, but that doesn't mean he couldn't have done it. You have to suspect everyone unless they have a good alibi. So far, the only people who were near the house are those we've listed. You've said they're all good people who couldn't possibly commit murder, but the fact is Mrs Milwood was poisoned. Somebody must have done it."

Connie sat still, her hands resting in her lap. "I'm sorry, I'm not terribly good at this."

Eliza reached over and squeezed her friend's hands. "It's not your fault. You know these people and have every right to like them. Except for Judith and Mr Wilson, I don't know anyone. It's easier for me."

Connie nodded. "I just don't believe any of them would do such a thing. It's one thing to dislike someone, but to murder them..." She shuddered and reached for the teapot to refill the cups.

"You're right, it's hard to imagine. I shouldn't have troubled you with this." Eliza folded up her paper. "Let's put this away and we can talk about something else. Tell me about the church. I hate to say it, but I should probably go to the service tomorrow. Will you be there to introduce me to everyone?"

"I'll be there, but I'm only introducing you if you promise to smile."

"What do you mean?"

Connie smirked. "You know perfectly well what I mean. You hate going to church and you're terrible at hiding it."

"Well, all those virtuous people thinking they know best. They've no idea."

Connie took her knitting from a bag and moved to a seat by the fire. "It looks like you'll be introducing yourself then."

"You wouldn't leave me." Eliza's eyes were wide.

"Not if you're on your best behaviour." Connie couldn't hide her grin any longer. "Just promise me you'll try to look interested. I have to see these people every week."

Eliza batted Connie's shoulder with the back of her hand. "You had me fooled then. I promise you'll come away proud of me."

The following morning, the Sunday service at church lived up to Eliza's expectations. As soon as she and Archie got home she abandoned her smile along with her wet umbrella in the hall, draped her coat over the stand and flounced onto the settee in the drawing room.

"What a dreadful service."

Archie handed her a sherry. "You'll have to get used to it. People will expect us to be there."

"I know and I'll do my duty, but what a waste of a morning. I'm not going to Evensong as well."

"How about once or twice a month?"

"Only if it means I get the morning off. There are so many other things I want to do. As soon as we've finished luncheon, I need you to get the medical books out."

Archie scowled at her. "What are you up to?"

"Call it idle curiosity."

"Has this inquisitiveness got anything to do with digitalis by any chance?"

Eliza allowed herself a small smile. "It might have, but what's wrong with that? Nobody else around here knows anything about it, and I doubt New Scotland Yard will either. I might as well do some research on it. At the moment, there doesn't seem to be a clear motive for Mrs Milwood's murder and no one seems capable of doing it. There's something not right with the timing of things as well. I want to check how quickly it gets into the body and when the first effects become noticeable."

"I've already reported that to the inquest."

"I know, and it all sounded fine, but..."

Archie's chin jutted forward. "But you think I've missed something?"

"Not necessarily, but I'd like to check. Besides, what else is there to do on a rainy Sunday afternoon?"

CHAPTER EIGHT

The Monday morning surgery passed uneventfully and once luncheon was over Eliza stood up from the dining table and reached for her handbag.

"I'm going round to Connie's. I didn't get much chance to speak to her yesterday."

Archie's forehead creased as he looked at his wife. "What do you mean, you didn't speak to her? You never left her side in church."

Eliza sighed. "Just because we were together, doesn't mean we could talk. Not properly. She was introducing me to everyone, that's different."

Archie shook his head and returned to his newspaper. "Oh, by the way, don't be late coming back. I've several house calls to make this afternoon and I may need some prescriptions making up. You still want to do the job, don't you?"

"Of course I do. Just don't prescribe anything too complicated for the time being, at least not anything I need to get my textbooks out for."

"Good grief, woman, I can't choose the illnesses they present to me."

Eliza reached over and kissed Archie on the forehead. "Don't get excited, I'm sure they'll have nothing that a course of codeine tablets won't solve. Isn't that what you usually start with?"

Eliza smiled but jumped out of the way as Archie flicked the newspaper at her.

"I'll give you some codeine tablets in a minute, if you're not careful. They may slow you down a bit!"

Eliza still had a grin on her face as she knocked on Connie's front door before letting herself in.

"It's only me. Oh, are you going out?" Her smile instantly disappeared.

"I hope so, it's a lovely day, but it's up to you," Connie said as Eliza studied her hat and coat. "I was waiting for you."

"How did you know I was coming?"

Connie shrugged. "Call it a hunch. You always finish luncheon around this time and I thought you might like a walk."

Eliza sighed. "Am I that predictable already?"

"Not really, but if you weren't here by quarter past, I would have had to come around to the surgery, so I thought I may as well get ready."

Eliza smirked. "I see you've got it all worked out. Do you know where I'd like to go?"

"Of course I do, you'd like to go to the same places I would. First of all, I thought we could do a lap of the village green. You haven't walked down to the far end yet, near the pond, and the ducks may be there."

Eliza smiled. She'd always enjoyed feeding the ducks

when she was younger. "You're right, I would like that. Lead the way."

"Have you found out anything else about the murder since yesterday?" Connie pulled the garden gate closed behind them.

"No, I'm no further on. You were right though; you wouldn't suspect any of them of being murderers. I suppose that's the benefit of puzzling over the events in the newspapers. Everyone's a stranger and you have no attachment to them. In a place like this where everyone knows everyone else, it's more difficult."

"Are you going to stick with the newspapers then?"

Eliza gave her friend a sideways glance. "Don't be silly. What's life without a challenge?"

The stroll around the pond only took twenty minutes and before long they were heading towards the police station.

"I wonder who they'll send from London to lead the investigation," Eliza said.

Connie pointed to a figure a little way ahead, walking towards them. "Why don't we ask Sergeant Cooper? He's a friendly sort. I'm sure he'll tell us anything he knows."

"Oh, I hope so. I'm at a disadvantage. The police can legitimately question all the suspects they like but I need to resort to being devious."

Connie didn't have time to answer before Sergeant Cooper was upon them.

"Good afternoon, ladies." The sergeant gave them a friendly salute. "A lovely day for a walk. How are you settling in, Mrs Thomson?"

"Very well, thank you, Sergeant. Mrs Appleton here's taking good care of me."

Connie flushed as the sergeant beamed at her. "And you couldn't wish for a nicer person to take you under her wing. I'm glad she's got you living next door to her now. A terrible time she's had with her husband dying and all."

Eliza suppressed a smile when she noticed the affection in the sergeant's eyes. "I'll take care of her. With a potential murderer in the village we can't be too careful."

The sergeant straightened his back. "A bad business that was, no doubt about it."

"Have you heard who'll be coming down from London to lead the inquiry?" Eliza asked. "We need the killer behind bars as soon as possible."

"That we do, but we had word this morning to say the inspector is otherwise engaged for the time being. Constable Jenkins and I are to start the inquiries before he gets here."

Eliza clapped her hands under her chin. "How exciting. I don't suppose you're used to dealing with murders in Moreton."

"No, this will be the first. We've been drawing up a plan of action this morning as it happens."

"Always a good place to start." Eliza smiled at him. "So who's on the list so far?"

Sergeant Cooper reached into his breast pocket and took out his police-issue pocket notepad. He flicked through several pages. "Well, as we see it, the obvious suspects are Mr or Mrs Wilson and we'll talk to them first."

"Yes, they should be a good help. Then who?"

The sergeant looked at her blankly. "Then who? Well, no one. We expect either Mr or Mrs Wilson did it, possibly both of them together. If we can get them to confess we shouldn't need to talk to anyone else."

Eliza gazed at the floor as she bit down on her lip. "What if it wasn't them?"

"Not them? But it must be…"

Eliza stared at the uncomprehending face of the sergeant. "Forgive me for interfering, but there were other people in the house, it might be worth talking to them too."

"Yes, of course. I'd better add them to the list." He licked his pencil and poised it over the paper. "Who would that be then?"

"Well, the son and daughter and the cook to start with, I would suggest."

"Yes, of course, although I can't see any of them doing it."

Eliza pursed her lips while she thought of a tactful response. In the silence, Connie interrupted.

"Mrs Thomson's interested in investigations like this. She often follows them in the newspaper and even helped the police in London to solve a murder earlier this year."

"Really?" The sergeant's eyes were wide.

"If we called round occasionally, would you keep us updated of what's going on?" Connie continued. "We're playing a little game to see if either of us can guess correctly who the murderer is."

The sergeant straightened his back and beamed at Connie. "I'm sure the station would be a lot nicer place if you two ladies called in on us more often. We'll be visiting Mr and Mrs Wilson in the morning. Why don't you call at this time tomorrow and I'll tell you how we get on?"

"That's very kind of you." Connie's cheeks coloured as the sergeant's eyes lingered on her.

"It's my pleasure. Now, I must get on, I'll see you tomorrow."

With Sergeant Cooper gone the two continued towards the church on their way back to the surgery.

"I'd say the sergeant has a soft spot for you." Eliza's eyes sparkled as she nudged her friend's arm.

"Get away with you, he's only being friendly."

"He'd like to be a lot more than friendly if you want my opinion."

Connie's blush deepened.

"You should be pleased, but even if you're not, can we make the most of it? He's going to be delighted every time you go to the station. Maybe we should make this walk a regular occurrence, at least until the murderer's caught."

"You mean you want me to encourage him?" Connie's eyes widened.

"Don't you like him?"

Connie focussed straight ahead as her cheeks once again coloured. "That's beside the point. I'm not long out of mourning."

Eliza softened her tone. "You're right, I'm sorry, but can we still call tomorrow? It is about business after all."

Connie glanced at her friend and nodded. "All right then, but don't go getting ideas, do you hear?"

CHAPTER NINE

The following afternoon, with the early summer sunshine brightening the blossom on the trees lining the sides of the road, Sergeant Cooper was waiting for them outside the police station.

"Good afternoon, Sergeant," Eliza said. "You look pleased with yourself."

The sergeant gazed at Connie with a twinkle in his eyes, before turning to Eliza.

"I was hoping you'd call. I took Constable Jenkins with me to see the Wilsons this morning. I'm not sure that we have much to tell you, but I wondered what you might make of it. Jenkins is putting the kettle on. Will you join us in a cup of tea?"

"That would be lovely, thank you." Eliza smiled at Sergeant Cooper as he escorted them into the back room of the police station.

Five minutes later, with the tea poured, the four of them sat around a small table as Sergeant Cooper took out his notepad.

"As I said, we visited Mr and Mrs Wilson this morning. I called as soon as I'd seen you yesterday and asked Mr Wilson to delay going into work so we could talk to him."

"That was a good idea," Eliza said. "Was he a help?"

"After a fashion. He didn't have much to say other than he'd been in work on the day Mrs Milwood died. He left home at half past seven that morning and walked to the workshop in Over Moreton."

"Did he take breakfast before he left?"

The sergeant nodded. "He did, in the dining room. Mrs Harris, the cook, had made kippers for him and his son Frank. They ate them together and then went straight out. Said he didn't go near the kitchen."

"And what about the night before his mother's death? What was he doing between midnight and seven o'clock?"

The two police officers looked at each other before the constable spoke. "Sleeping, I would say."

"But you didn't check?" Eliza's eyes flicked between the two of them. "We heard at the inquest that the poison could have been given any time after one o'clock in the morning."

The sergeant turned to a new page in his pad to scribble a few words.

"What about Mrs Wilson?" Eliza asked. "Did she have anything new to add to her testimony at the inquest?"

"Anything new?" The sergeant frowned as he flicked through his notes. "Let me see. She said Mrs Milwood was taken ill in the morning and she had put her to bed at about half past eleven." He turned the page. "She looked in on her around one o'clock and when she found her asleep, she went out."

"Yes, she mentioned that at the inquest."

The sergeant fumbled to turn over the next page. "She said she came and sat on a bench near the bowling green and that you two ladies joined her. You stayed with her for about half an hour before you walked back to the surgery together and she headed across the green to go home."

Connie nodded. "Yes, that's right."

"Yes ... right ... well, she didn't go into the bedroom straight away because she thought Mrs Milwood would still be asleep. It was about half past four when she eventually found the body but she noticed the bedcovers were soiled and so she cleaned them up. By the time she'd done that, Mr Wilson was home, and he came straight for Dr Thomson."

Eliza took a deep breath. "Did you ask her anything about what Mrs Milwood had eaten or drunk since the night before ... or who'd prepared the food for her? We've assumed it was the cook, but was it?"

Again the sergeant said nothing but made another note in his pad.

"Did you ask about Mrs Milwood's medication? When did she take her last dose of codeine ... or any of the medicines in the cabinet?"

When the sergeant kept writing, Eliza turned to Constable Jenkins.

"Constable, did you examine the doors or windows to see if any had been forced? So far, we've assumed the murderer came from within the house, but what if it was someone from outside the family? From what I understand she wasn't a popular woman."

When Jenkins did nothing but stare at his sergeant, Eliza stood up and turned her back to the table, taking a deep breath as she did. "I don't suppose you spoke to the cook, or either of the children?"

"Erm ... we didn't see them, did we, Sarge?"

Eliza was on her third deep breath when Connie sprang up from the table.

"I know. Eliza wants us to visit Mrs Wilson tomorrow. If you don't mind, Sergeant, we could ask her these questions and report back to you. It would save you having to go back and she may feel more comfortable talking to us."

Eliza turned around with a smile. "What a marvellous idea."

"Yes, indeed." The sergeant took out his handkerchief and mopped his brow. "That would be most helpful of you. We have so much else to do around here, don't we, Jenkins?"

"Yes, yes, we do, but we'll write up the evidence to give to the inspector if you like. Split the workload with you."

"Do you know yet when the inspector's arriving?" Eliza asked.

The sergeant put his notepad back in his breast pocket. "They've said it'll be another couple of days but haven't confirmed it. I don't think we're a priority. If we could get the culprit locked up before he arrives, it might be best all round. We don't want him here poking his nose into things that don't concern him."

CHAPTER TEN

E liza was downstairs early the following morning, but was frustrated to find Archie in no hurry to finish his breakfast.

"Are you going to be long with that?" She nodded towards the toast on her husband's plate. "You'll have patients waiting for you."

Archie checked the clock. "It's not nine o'clock yet. If they choose to be early, it's not my fault."

"Well, you have a dozen appointments. Will you not spend an extra ten minutes talking to each patient on top of their actual consultation?"

Archie's brow creased as he studied his wife. "Why, what's the rush?"

"I need to get away promptly at the end of surgery, but your mornings seem to be getting longer."

"I need to get to know everyone. Isn't that what country doctors do? Know their patients on first-name terms?"

"You don't need to know them all in the first week." Eliza folded her napkin and laid it on the table while Archie took a final bite from his toast and washed it down with the remains of his cup of tea.

"Why are you in such a hurry, anyway?"

"Me and Connie are visiting Judith later ... on official police business."

Archie raised his eyebrows. "Official police business? Does the sergeant know about this?"

Eliza stood up and hovered around the table. "Of course he does; he was the one who asked us to help. He visited Judith yesterday with that young constable, but between the two of them they only found out what we already knew from the inquest. There are so many other questions that need answering and frankly they're not up to the task. Not that it's their fault, they've never had to investigate a murder before, but they're totally out of their depth. The inspector's due from London in a day or two and they'd like some answers for when he arrives."

"And so they asked you to help?"

"They did as it happens. I wouldn't do it otherwise." Eliza reached for her handbag. "Now, will you get a move on? I've told Cook I'd like luncheon on the table at noon."

Mercifully, Archie kept his consultations brief and by half past twelve Eliza had her coat on, ready to collect Connie.

"You're early," Connie said as she opened the door.

"I know, but I've got so many questions I'm itching to get started."

"Judith won't have finished luncheon yet. We need to leave it until at least one o'clock."

"You're right." Eliza walked to the window and looked out

towards the Wilsons' house. After a moment she beckoned for Connie to join her.

"Isn't that Mrs Harris walking across the green?"

Connie studied the figure in the distance. "You're right, it is, they must be finished luncheon early today. Oh, wait a moment, what day is it? Of course, it's Wednesday, her afternoon off. They'll have had luncheon early. Mrs Harris doesn't like being delayed any longer than necessary."

Eliza watched Mrs Harris for a moment longer. "She looks like she's taking the path to the shop, or the church. If we go now, we'll miss her. It could be a stroke of good fortune her being out of the house. There'll be no chance of her listening to us from the other side of the door."

"You do say some funny things. Of course she wouldn't do that. I think Dr Thomson's right about you reading too much."

"We'll see." Eliza gave Connie a sideways glance before heading for the door.

Five minutes later, Eliza knocked on the Wilsons' front door and stepped back to wait for it to be opened.

"How lovely to see you both." Judith beckoned them in. "Come through to the sunroom. I was expecting to spend another afternoon on my own and I've lifted my embroidery out."

"We hope we're not interrupting, but we thought you might like some company," Connie said.

Judith smiled. "When Mother was alive, I used to dream of having afternoons to myself, but now I have them, well, it isn't quite what I was expecting."

"No, take it from me, it's so much nicer having company," Connie said.

They followed Judith into a bright room filled with plants.

"We have a confession to make though," Eliza said. "We understand you had Sergeant Cooper and the constable round yesterday."

"We did. Is there a problem?"

"Only in so far as we'd hoped they'd find out more from you than we'd already learned from the inquest. We spoke to the sergeant yesterday afternoon, and it seems they didn't ask the right questions."

"They tried, bless them, but no, they didn't," Judith said. "They only asked where me and Joseph had been on the afternoon Mother died and so we told them. Are you here to try again?"

"You could say that. The thing is, if you didn't poison Mrs Milwood, then somebody else did, and if we're going to clear your name, we need to find out who."

Judith's face paled. "That's what scares me."

"Why would it scare you?" Connie had made herself comfortable in a seat next to Judith. "You've no need to be frightened if you've done nothing wrong."

"No, of course not ... I'll tell you what, let me get you some tea."

"Are you no closer to getting a maid?" Eliza asked.

Judith sighed. "My mind hasn't been on it for a few days, but I placed an advertisement in the paper yesterday. The sooner we get someone the better."

"Why did your old maid leave?"

"Ruby? I wish I knew. One day she was here and the next she wasn't, and the only person who didn't seem surprised was Mother."

Eliza raised an eyebrow. "Didn't they get on?"

"They did when she first joined us. Ruby's a nice girl, not

your average domestic help, and she was always cheerful. I assumed they'd had a disagreement."

"But you've no idea what?"

Judith shook her head. "I tried several times to ask Mother about it, but you saw how she was. If she didn't want to talk about something, you couldn't get a word out of her. Most of the time she was only interested in talking about herself."

"Maybe Ruby tired of being here."

Judith sighed. "That wouldn't surprise me, although fortunately for her, she didn't have much to do with her."

Connie gazed into the distance. "She was a nice girl. I remember meeting her several times in the shop; she was always polite. Could you ask her to come back?"

"I wish I could, but there's no point. By all accounts, she's got a much better position at the manor house in Over Moreton. She wouldn't want to come back here."

Eliza shifted in her seat. "What about your daughter? Doesn't she still live with you?"

"Flora? Yes, she's upstairs."

"Has she been helping you around the house?"

Judith rolled her eyes. "You'd expect her to, wouldn't you? Unfortunately, she couldn't bear to be in the same room as Mother and spends most of her days in the attic. She only comes down for her meals."

"That doesn't sound normal." A frown creased Eliza's forehead.

"No, but she was determined to keep out of her grandmother's way. Mother couldn't manage the stairs, you see."

"Did Flora dislike her so much?"

Judith nodded. "Oh yes, it's been a difficult time. You

learned the hard way what Mother thought of educating women. Well, Flora's been determined to go to university since she was twelve. She's a clever girl and got first-class honours in all her school exams. When we lived in London, it was all she talked about, but as soon as we came here Mother told her, in no uncertain terms, that she wouldn't waste any money on her Flora's education."

"Poor thing," Eliza said. "I know you said Mrs Milwood was the one with the money, but couldn't Mr Wilson have paid? He still works, doesn't he?"

Judith gave a sarcastic laugh and wandered over to the full-height window that looked out over the garden. "Before we moved, Joseph had a good position, and a good salary, in London, but when we came here, the best offer he had was for a position in a workshop, of all places. He's a chartered accountant and yet the wages he gets working in Over Moreton are a pittance compared with what he earned in London. Within months he was relying on Mother and she soon realised it was her way of keeping us here."

"But you still wanted to leave?"

Judith turned her back on her guests. "I did, but Joseph wouldn't hear of it. She'd told him that if we so much as thought of leaving, she'd disinherit us."

Eliza's mouth dropped open, and she turned to Connie.

"But Mr Wilson's an only child?" Connie said.

"That made no difference to her. She'd inherited a great deal of money from her second husband and with money comes power. A power she loved to use." The distaste in Judith's voice was unmistakable.

"So she was effectively blackmailing Mr Wilson to stay here?"

"If you want to put it like that, then yes, I suppose so."

Eliza paused and took a deep breath before she spoke. "So Mr Wilson had quite a motive to get rid of his mother?"

Judith's eyes were wide as she spun around to stare at Eliza. "No, of course not. He wouldn't hear a word against her."

"So you don't think he'd poison his mother to collect his inheritance and take you all back to London."

"Oh Eliza, please don't say that, of course he wouldn't. I can't even bear the thought of that happening."

Eliza studied her friend. "Have you spoken to him about it?"

"I don't need to. I'm a light sleeper and I know he was beside me the whole time the night before she died. The following morning, he was up as usual, had breakfast and left for work. He wouldn't have hurt her. Please believe me."

Eliza studied Judith as she turned back to the window.

"I'm sorry, I didn't mean to upset you. I'll tell you what, shall I ask Cook to make us that pot of tea?"

"We saw... ow!" Connie yelped as Eliza kicked her under the table.

"It's her afternoon off." Judith continued to stare out of the window and failed to notice Connie rubbing her ankle. "I'll go."

"No, don't be silly. Connie will, won't you?" Eliza gestured for Connie to make the tea.

Connie scowled at Eliza but stood up when Eliza mouthed *Please* to her.

Once they were alone, Eliza walked to the window to join Judith. "I hope you don't mind me asking, but did Mrs Milwood leave a will?"

"She did." Judith spoke without turning around. "By chance, her solicitor called on Friday afternoon to see her. He hadn't heard the news but had a copy of the will with him. He ran through it with Joseph but took it back to London. Except for a few legacies Joseph will inherit everything."

"I expect he'll need to show it to the police at some point. I'll ask Sergeant Cooper to write to the inspector who's coming down here. He can check it while he's in London." Eliza paused to gauge Judith's reaction but when she didn't stir, Eliza continued.

"You do realise it appears to give Mr Wilson another motive for the murder? If we're to clear his name, we'll need to talk to him. Is he at work?"

"No, Mr Royal has been very good and given him a few days to get his affairs in order. He's gone to the undertaker's to discuss the funeral."

"You know you won't be able to bury her until the police release the body?" Eliza rested a hand on Judith's arm.

"I do, but arrangements still have to be made." Judith wiped her eyes on her handkerchief. "I'm sorry, give me a minute and I'll be fine."

Eliza wandered back to her chair before changing the subject. "Why did your eldest son leave home? Did Mrs Milwood make his life miserable too?"

"Quite probably but whatever happened, nobody told me or Joseph. I've not seen Sam for weeks; he didn't even turn up at the inquest." Judith continued to dab her eyes with a handkerchief. "Thank goodness I still have Frank here."

"Does he work locally too?"

"He's learning to become a reporter with the local newspaper. He was out early on the morning of Mother's death and didn't come home until late. As far as I can tell, he had no argument with her." Judith followed Eliza back across the room and slumped into the nearest chair. "What a mess. I know I shouldn't say this, but I can't say I'm sorry she's dead. I just wish she'd died of natural causes so we didn't have to deal with all this."

Eliza patted Judith's shoulder. "Connie will be here in a minute with that tea. I'll put an extra sugar in for you. Tell me, does Cook take every Wednesday afternoon off?"

"Yes, why?" Judith looked up.

"I just wondered. I remember you told the inquest she was out on the afternoon Mrs Milwood died. Do you know what she does on her afternoons off?"

Judith shook her head. "No. It's the sort of information she doesn't volunteer and I never ask."

"So did Cook get along with Mrs Milwood?"

"Yes, I think so although there was something of an atmosphere between them these last few weeks. My guess is that after Ruby left, Cook had more chores to do but Mother wasn't in any hurry to get a new maid. You must call one day when she's here. I'm sure she'll tell you."

"I will." Eliza ran her finger over the leaf of a large plant situated to the side of her chair. "Tell me, what did Cook make Mrs Milwood for breakfast on the morning she died?"

Judith shrugged. "Nothing she could poison. Mother always had two softly boiled eggs and a slice of bread and butter."

"And to drink?"

"A cup of tea, but that would have been out of the shared pot."

"And she had nothing else?"

"No, not that I'm aware of."

"What about the night before? Did she eat the same meal as the rest of you?"

"She will have done. It was a Tuesday and so we had a bit of liver with potatoes. As a family we always ate the same meal. She would have had a cup of tea from the shared pot that night too."

Eliza stood up to pace the room. "So there was no opportunity for anyone to slip anything into her food or drinks?"

"No, I wouldn't think so."

"Something's not right. There are obviously people who had a motive for wanting Mrs Milwood dead, but there was no opportunity. We've established she died due to an overdose of digitalis, but we don't know when it was given or where it came from. Dr Thomson has some in the surgery, but since the inquest I've checked the bottles and there doesn't appear to be any missing. Certainly not enough to kill anyone. Are you sure she didn't have a supply in the house?"

"Quite sure. You saw for yourself that she couldn't go outside alone and so if she ever needed to go to the doctor's or collect any medicine, I was always with her. I'd know if there were any in the house."

"There was a tonic wine and some herbal medicine in the cupboard when I first looked. Do you know if she took them often?"

Judith shrugged. "Not that I'm aware of. The bottles in the cupboard have been there for a while and they're still quite full."

"Did you say she didn't take either the tonic wine or herbal medicine on the morning she died?"

Judith put her hands to her mouth. "I did, but I forgot to tell you. I remembered after you'd gone that she asked for some tonic wine when she was feeling sickly."

"And you gave it to her?"

"No, that's why I forgot. I helped her to the kitchen, and she took some herself before I took her to her room."

Eliza paused. "Do you mind if I take another look in the cupboard? The digitalis must have come from somewhere and I'm wondering if the murderer slipped some into one of the bottles."

"Feel free. Mrs Harris won't be there to question you."

"Here we are, a nice pot of tea," Connie said as she pushed the door open with her foot. "I hope you don't mind, Judith, but there was a cake in the pantry that looked delicious and so I've brought it in."

"Of course I don't mind. I'll say that for Mrs Harris, she does make a nice cake."

"While you pour the tea, I'll nip to the kitchen and check those bottles." Eliza stood up and was out of the room before Judith could respond. She found her way to the kitchen and headed straight to the medicine cabinet.

Within seconds she'd unlocked the door and pulled a cork from the bottle of tonic wine. It released a hint of citrus aromas and she put her nose to the bottle. *It smells all right.* She glanced around for a glass and poured out a small amount. *No evidence of dried digitalis leaves.* Mindful that the liquid could be poisonous, she wet her lips with a tiny amount. *Nothing bitter about that.* She picked up the herbal medicine and took off the lid. It was almost full. *No point testing that.* With a sigh, she slipped the bottle of tonic wine into the pocket of her dress. She might as well take it home and hope that Archie could work out what was in it. Judith wouldn't mind.

Now, what else do we have in here? Eliza worked her way along the wall from cupboard to cupboard before opening the pantry door and stepping inside. *Nothing.* She stood with her hands on her hips surveying the packets of flour and sugar, cooked meats, bread and bottles of gin. The cook clearly enjoyed the odd tipple. After studying the contents for a full minute she turned to leave. The murderer must have brought their own digitalis and either used it all or taken the rest away with them.

By the time Eliza returned to the sunroom, Connie had poured the tea and a slice of cake was waiting for her. She pulled the bottle of tonic wine from her pocket.

"I'd like to take this away for testing. I don't think there's anything in it, but given Mrs Milwood had some only hours before her death, it would be as well to check it."

Judith nodded. "I don't suppose I'll need it."

"I wondered as well, do you keep the doors and windows locked at night? We've assumed Mrs Milwood was poisoned by someone in the house, but there is the possibility of there being an intruder."

Judith immediately looked up. "It's funny you should say that, Joseph said the same thing last night."

"He did?" Eliza put down the cake she had just picked up. "Why would he do that?"

Judith flushed. "I'm sorry, I should have mentioned it earlier. Joseph said that when he left home that morning, the front door was unlocked. He swore he locked it the night before and asked if I'd been out that morning."

"Which you hadn't?" Eliza raised an eyebrow.

"No. We checked around the front step for any sign of force but couldn't find anything. We came to the conclusion that Joseph must have forgotten to lock it."

"Does that mean anyone from the village could have murdered her then?" Connie asked.

Eliza sat back in her chair. "In theory it does, although it still doesn't explain how they gave her enough digitalis to kill her without waking up the whole house." She turned back to face Judith. "Had anything in the bedroom been disturbed when you found her?"

"Nothing that was obvious." Judith paused to think. "Although, now you mention it, she normally took a glass of water to bed with her, but on the morning she became ill, it wasn't there. We'd assumed she'd forgotten it the previous evening and so I fetched a fresh one for her."

"Assuming she hadn't forgotten it, who might have moved it?"

Judith shrugged. "Nobody. I was the only one who went into her room, and it wasn't me. Flora wouldn't go in unless she was told to, and Cook was the same."

"What about Mr Wilson or Frank?"

Judith shook her head. "No. Even if they'd called in to see her, which would have been most unlikely, they wouldn't have thought to move a glass."

Eliza chewed on her lip. "All right, I need to think about this and come back to speak to everyone. This isn't as straightforward as I'd expected."

CHAPTER ELEVEN

Eliza and Connie left the Wilsons' house in silence and didn't speak until they reached the junction of the road around the village.

"Where to now?" Connie asked. "Are you up to going to the police station or do you want to go home?"

Eliza stopped and gazed up the road to her right. "If I'm being honest, I'd like to go home, but we did promise the sergeant we'd call in and so I suppose we should. We can give him an idea of what Judith said. There wasn't much that was new."

"Other than the fact that everyone held a grudge against Mrs Milwood, she was blackmailing Mr Wilson, the front door was unlocked and the water glass was missing," Connie said. "Not to mention anything you found out while I was making the tea."

Eliza stared at her friend. "Gracious, you were paying attention. I'm sorry about your ankle."

Connie scowled. "I should think so, what was that all about?"

"I wanted to ask Judith if Mrs Milwood had made a will and I thought it would be better if the two of us were alone."

"Hmm, a likely story. I'm sure she would have told me. What did she say?"

"There is a will, but Mr Wilson's put it away for safekeeping."

"Did he inherit everything?"

Eliza nodded. "Except for a few legacies. I don't suppose it should surprise us, but it was worth checking. We'd better tell Sergeant Cooper that as well. Come on, let's go. Do you want to tell him?"

"Me? Of course not."

Eliza laughed. "All right, I'll ask your opinion from time to time then."

Constable Jenkins was manning the desk when they arrived and he showed them into the sergeant's office.

"Good afternoon, ladies," he said, standing up. "Please, take a seat. I was hoping you'd call. I have some news for you."

Connie beamed at him. "We have some news for you too."

"Well then, I'm doubly glad you called. Now, ladies first, what did you want to tell me?"

Eliza told Sergeant Cooper about their afternoon with Judith. "It's not much to go on, but at least there are plenty of people with a motive. What did you have to say to us?"

"Well, we haven't been idle. Constable Jenkins and I paid a visit to several of the Wilsons' neighbours. Most said they hadn't seen or heard anything, but Mrs Petty seems to have been more alert than most."

"Which one's Mrs Petty?" Eliza looked to Connie.

"She's an elderly lady who lives on the corner on the main road. In a way it's next door to the Wilsons' but they're round the corner from each other. I think her garden runs across the bottom of the Wilsons'."

"Indeed it does." The sergeant's eyes sparkled as he smiled at Connie.

"Is she the nosy one you were telling me about?"

The sergeant grinned. "You could say that, but people like Mrs Petty are the sort we like. They make very good informants. Anyway, it seems your move into the village was on her list of things to pay attention to. She said she watched the removals men taking your belongings into the house."

Eliza cocked her head to one side. "I'm surprised the surgery's visible from that far away."

"It is a distance, but her house is almost directly opposite the surgery with only the village green between you. She says she has keen eyesight, and it surprised her that young Samuel Wilson was helping them out."

"Sam?" Eliza said.

"Shouldn't he have been at work?" Connie said almost at the same time.

"That's what we thought, but there's more." The sergeant puffed out his chest. "Young Flora was with him. He stopped to talk to her before disappearing back into the surgery while she walked home across the green."

Connie's cheeks flushed red.

"What's the matter?" Eliza asked.

"The sergeant's right. She was outside the surgery, I saw her too, although not with Sam. I didn't think to mention it because it was a couple of days before Mrs Milwood died."

Eliza glanced from Connie to the sergeant. "Would there be anything unusual about her being outside the surgery if she hadn't been with Sam?"

Connie shrugged. "I suppose not, but you rarely see her out in the afternoon, she's usually too busy with her books."

"And this Mrs Petty was sure it was Sam?"

Sergeant Cooper nodded. "I double-checked with her, and she was adamant. She prides herself on knowing what's going on and she's usually right."

"Someone needs to speak to Flora and Sam then," Eliza said. "Frank too."

Sergeant Cooper shifted in his seat. "We're happy to speak to the boys, but, well, it might be easier for you ladies to talk to a young girlie like Flora. Would you mind?"

Eliza beamed. "Of course not, we'll call tomorrow. Will you try and speak to the boys then as well?"

The smile returned to the sergeant's face. "We'll try but Mrs Petty had one other piece of information we want to follow up first. She said Mr Hewitt, the churchwarden, had called at the house the evening before Mrs Milwood's death."

"Yes, we knew that."

"The thing you might not know is that shortly after he left, she was in the garden and overheard an argument between Mr and Mrs Wilson about going back to London. She couldn't hear exactly what was said but thought Mr Hewitt's name was mentioned."

"Why would they argue about Mr Hewitt?" Connie asked.

"That's something we need to find out, but I'd say the argument about London is more relevant. After what you've told me, I'd lay odds that one or both of them murdered Mrs Milwood so they could get away from here."

Eliza sighed; it was certainly a possibility. "Let's not jump to conclusions. You speak to Mr Hewitt and we'll find Flora and report back tomorrow."

CHAPTER TWELVE

With the morning surgery and luncheon once again over, Eliza stood up from the dining table and planted a kiss on Archie's forehead.

"What's that for?" he asked, looking up from some correspondence.

"I'm going out."

"Again? I left some prescriptions in the dispensary that need making up."

Eliza sighed. "And I'll do them as soon as I get back from Judith's. There's nothing urgent, is there?"

"What's so urgent that Judith can't wait? I'm sure she can put the kettle on again once you arrive."

"It's not a social visit." Eliza straightened her back and looked down at Archie. "Sergeant Cooper's going to speak to Sam and Frank this afternoon, but he wasn't comfortable talking to Flora and asked us to do it."

Archie put the letter he was holding onto the table. "As long as you're sure Sergeant Cooper knows of this."

"As long as you're sure Sergeant Cooper knows of this."

"Of course he does. Now, I'd better go, Connie will be wondering where I am."

"Obviously," Archie muttered to himself as he returned to his letter.

By the time Eliza reached next door, Connie was waiting for her wearing a new summer hat that matched the royal blue of her skirt.

"You're looking very smart," Eliza said. "I need to get myself some new hats. I've had this one for years." She tapped the rim of her straw bonnet. "The flowers on it are looking rather tatty."

"They look fine to me. You're not comparing yourself to London society women now."

Eliza sighed. "You're right, but I need to keep up to date, at the very least for when we visit Father. Perhaps we can go up to London to do some shopping once we find our murderer."

Connie smiled. "I'd love to, but it'll be you spending the money. When do I need the latest fashions?"

"You never know when you might get a fancy invitation."

"Well, when I do, they'd better give me enough time to go shopping."

Eliza chuckled as Connie pulled the front door closed behind them and they started down the garden path.

"I hope Judith doesn't mind us talking to Flora," Eliza said. "We don't want her to think we're accusing her daughter of being a murderer."

"I'm sure she won't." Connie hesitated once they reached the gate. "Actually, before we go, do you mind if we nip to the shop? I've run out of sugar and I don't want to forget it."

"Why didn't you get it this morning?"

"I forgot and only realised at luncheon."

"As long as Archie doesn't see me heading in that direction. He's got a few prescriptions for me to do and was moaning about me coming out this afternoon as it was."

"I'm sorry, I'll be as quick as I can." Connie set off at pace towards the shop.

"It's all right, you don't need to walk that fast, the prescriptions aren't urgent. I'm sure he was only trying to stop me being involved with the case."

"He doesn't need them for this afternoon's visits?"

"No, we've set up a system so that unless they're urgent, patients pick them up the following day. I can do them later."

Connie smirked. "That's a relief. I wasn't sure how far I could walk at that speed."

They hurried past the surgery and were almost at the shop when Connie nudged Eliza.

"There's Flora." She nodded towards a young girl who was leaving the shop.

Eliza studied the girl walking towards them. The wide rim of the young girl's hat cast a shadow across her face.

"She looks rather overdressed for a Thursday afternoon in Moreton-on-Thames." Eliza admired the wide sleeves of her blouse and long, flowing skirt. "She looks like she's practising for London society."

"Good afternoon, Flora," Connie said as they drew closer. "It's not often we see you at the shop."

Pale blue eyes peered out at them from under the hat. "Mother sent me. Now we're without a maid, she says I must do more to help."

"And quite right too," Eliza said.

Flora stared at the stranger and ran her eyes up and down

her tailored dress suit. "Are you Mrs Thomson, the doctor's wife?"

Eliza nodded. "I am."

Flora's face broke into a smile. "You went to university, didn't you? Which one did you go to?"

"Bedford College in London. It was a few years ago now though."

"I want to go there. What did you study?"

"Science."

"You must tell me all about it, I want to study medicine." Flora was almost bouncing on the spot. "It would be really helpful if you'd speak to Mother and Father and tell them how good it is. Thankfully, it looks like we'll be moving back to London soon enough, although I want to live in a room near the university if I can."

"So you're moving?" Connie asked.

Flora's eyes lit up. "We will be, although they haven't admitted it yet. Now Grandmother's dead, there's no point staying around here, is there?"

Eliza tilted her head to one side. "You don't seem very upset about your grandmother."

"Upset?" Eliza detected a certain glee in the young girl's eyes. "Why would I be upset? Grandmother was horrible. She wouldn't pay for me to go to university. She said women should stay at home and look after their husbands and children and houses. She had no idea how times have changed."

Eliza raised an eyebrow. "You can't be happy about her death."

Flora shrugged. "It happens to us all, eventually. She was old."

"You know someone poisoned her?"

"Yes, Mother told me. It's not the way I would have murdered her though. I would have taken a heavy stick and..."

"That's enough," Eliza said. "You've just told us you want to study medicine, a profession designed to heal people and here you are talking about *killing* someone."

"I was only saying *how* I would have done it, not that I *would* have. There's a difference."

"That's beside the point. The police will need to find the killer before you can move back to London."

Flora's eyes narrowed as she looked from Connie to Eliza. "No, surely not. You mean Sergeant Cooper and Constable Jenkins? How are they going to find a poisoner? I bet they'd never even heard of digitalis before Grandmother's death, let alone know what it is."

"But you do?" Connie raised an eyebrow at her.

"Of course I do, they wouldn't accept me to study medicine if I didn't. Well, the police had better hurry up, I need to be back in London for September."

Flora turned to leave, but as she did Eliza caught her arm. "Please, don't go. I'm hoping we can help each other. We want to find the killer as much as you do and so we're helping the police with their investigations. Could we ask you a few questions to see if we can speed things up?"

"You're helping them ... why?"

"You said yourself, the police aren't familiar with poisons and so I offered to help. They were part of my course at university."

Flora nodded. "That makes sense, although I won't be able to tell you much."

"You may know more than you think. We've been told Mr

99

Hewitt the churchwarden called at the house on the evening before your grandmother died. Do you have any idea why?"

Flora shook her head. "I didn't even know he'd been to the house until I heard the front door slam and I looked out the window to see him leaving."

"Would that be the window in the attic? Are you able to see the garden path from that angle?"

Although the bowling pavilion blocked the view, Flora glanced in the direction of the house. "I can see the gate and I watched him pull it closed behind him."

"Are you sure you heard nothing while he was there? This could be important."

"No, I didn't, but ... well, once he'd gone I went downstairs to speak to Mother, but she was in the drawing room with Grandmother."

"Did you go in?" Connie asked.

Flora shuddered. "I didn't. The two of them were having a right argument, shouting at each other and everything. Before you ask, I don't know what they were arguing about because I immediately turned around and went back upstairs."

"Did they argue often?" Connie asked.

Flora rolled her eyes. "*All* the time, but I don't blame Mother. Grandmother constantly said things to upset her."

Eliza nodded, but when Flora became quiet, she changed the subject. "Can I ask you about something else? We've had reports that on the Monday before the murder, on the day I moved into the village in fact, you were outside the surgery with your brother Sam."

Flora's face hardened as her eyes narrowed. "Well, whoever told you that is lying. You said yourself I rarely go out, and Sam would have been at work. It's nothing but idle gossip."

"But I saw..." Connie's words were cut off as the church bells struck one o'clock.

"Gosh, is that the time?" Flora said. "I must be going. I'm sorry I can't be any more help, but I really don't pay attention to what's going on around here. Good day to you."

Before Eliza could stop her, Flora turned and hurried towards the footpath that ran across the green.

"What was that about?" Eliza said once Flora was out of earshot.

"I've no idea, but she was lying. Why would she do that?"

"You're sure it was her you saw?" Eliza asked.

"Positive, and judging by her reaction I would say she's hiding something. She knows a lot more about that afternoon than she's telling us."

Eliza's gaze followed the rapidly disappearing shape of Flora. "I would say so, but what? Is she protecting someone? Sam perhaps ... or does she have something of her own to hide? She certainly seemed full of herself when she was talking about poisoning her grandmother."

"Judith would have been horrified if she'd heard her."

Eliza pursed her lips. "It adds another layer of complexity, that's for sure. Anyway, now we no longer need to go to the Wilsons' house, shall we call on Sergeant Cooper and ask how he's getting on?"

"Aren't we a bit early?"

"Probably, but at least we can ask if he's had the chance to talk to Sam yet. Maybe we should go and find him if he hasn't."

Sergeant Cooper was at the desk when they arrived, but

his usual cheerful disposition had disappeared. He didn't even have a smile for Connie.

"Good afternoon, Sergeant," Eliza said. "Have we come at a bad time?"

The sergeant glanced over his shoulder and kept his voice down when he spoke. "It's not the best time. Can you come back tomorrow?"

"As you wish," Eliza said, "but before we go, can we ask if you've called to see Sam Wilson yet?"

"Sam?" The sergeant looked momentarily confused. "Oh, no. We didn't get there this morning and then we got interrupted." He peered again over his shoulder. "We'll try and go tomorrow."

"If you're busy, we could go for you?"

"Sergeant Cooper, can I ... oh, I do apologise, ladies." A man of medium build with dark hair and a pencil-thin moustache appeared from the office behind the counter. "I didn't realise Sergeant Cooper was dealing with you."

"Ah, yes," the sergeant managed. "Inspector, this is Mrs Thomson and Mrs Appleton. Ladies, this is Inspector Adams from New Scotland Yard."

"Charmed, I'm sure, ladies," Inspector Adams said. "Are you having a spot of bother?"

"No, not at all, Inspector," Eliza said. "We came to see Sergeant Cooper about the death of Mrs Milwood. We have some information for him."

"I'm sure that's most helpful of you." The smile on the inspector's face failed to reach his eyes. "Why don't you tell me and I'll deal with it from here?"

"Well, it's nothing much," Eliza said. "We've been talking to young Flora Wilson, the deceased's granddaughter, and she said she wasn't outside the surgery on Monday afternoon."

"Thank you, ladies, but the victim wasn't murdered until Wednesday and she was found in her own bed." Inspector Adams walked around the counter to escort them out, the smirk remaining on his face. "Now, if you'd like to run along, Sergeant Cooper has a murderer to catch."

"And we've been helping him." Connie's brow creased.

"Judging by the current lack of evidence, I very much doubt it." The inspector glared at Sergeant Cooper. "There's a reason they post police officers to these rural villages, and it isn't because of their detective skills. I'll be taking charge from now on and we should finally get some answers."

The smile fell from Eliza's lips as she glowered at the inspector. "Is this what they teach you in London? How to patronise and belittle those trying to help you? I'd wager you've no idea of the significance of Monday afternoon or the work we've done with Sergeant Cooper. Well, if you see us as nothing more than interfering women with nothing better to do, you can work it out for yourself and see how far you get. Come along, Connie."

Eliza stormed out the door leaving Connie momentarily rooted to the spot.

"What a horrible man," she said when she caught Eliza up.

"Horrible, indeed." Eliza didn't slow her stride. "They wouldn't have a clue what was going on if it wasn't for us and that's how he talks to us. Well, if he thinks he's getting any more help from me, he can think again."

"Are you going to stop your inquiries?"

"I most certainly am not. Judith asked for help, and help

we will, but he'll only find out about it when we tell them who the murderer is. There's no chance they'll work it out for themselves."

Connie gasped for breath as she tried to keep up with Eliza, but finally when they reached the front gate of the surgery, Eliza stopped and put a hand on Connie's shoulder.

"I'm sorry, my dear." She glared back in the direction of the police station. "He made me so mad. Will you join me for a cup of tea? I swear if I go inside alone, something's likely to get broken."

Connie recoiled, her eyes wide, causing Eliza to laugh. "Oh dear, what do I sound like? Don't worry, I promise I won't lay a finger on you. That inspector, on the other hand, I could smack across the face."

"Please don't do that, they'll lock you up."

Eliza's shoulders slumped. "You're right, of course. Oh, it's so unfair."

"What, that you can't help them?"

"No, that I can't give him a clip around the ear." Noticing the shock on Connie's face, Eliza put an arm around her shoulder. "Oh Connie, dear, please don't worry. You should know me by now; I'm all talk. As much as I might like to do something to him I never would. Come on in and let's get that cup of tea."

They walked towards the front door, but when they were halfway up the path Connie stopped. "Oh, for goodness' sake, I need to go back. I never did get that sugar."

CHAPTER THIRTEEN

Eliza held the newspaper in front of her and shook it sharply to fold it down its centre line. Archie looked up from his seat at the dining table.

"Must you make such a noise? I'm trying to concentrate."

Eliza gritted her teeth. "I'm sorry, the paper wouldn't fold properly."

"There are quieter ways to fold a newspaper."

A knock on the front door distracted them and a moment later, Iris showed Connie in.

"Oh, I'm sorry, I thought you'd be finished by now." Connie stared at the empty plates on the dining table as Iris loaded them onto a tray.

"There's no need to rush, is there?" Eliza couldn't keep the frustration from her voice.

"Will you calm down?" Archie said. "I told you to leave it to the police,"

Eliza waited for Iris to leave the room. "If we'd left it to the police we'd know no more now than we knew after the inquest. They've no idea."

"They're trying their best," Connie said.

"Maybe they are, but ... never mind, what's done is done. Come and sit down. Now we've got Archie's attention, I want to quiz him about the time of death in relation to the time the poison was given."

"I thought you knew that," Connie said.

"And I thought the inspector told you to keep out of the police inquiry," Archie added.

"I'm not doing this for the police, I'm doing it for Judith. She asked me to help and I don't care what the inspector says, he can't stop me from helping a friend. If he doesn't want to know what we find out, it's his loss, not mine."

Archie sighed. "What do you want to know?"

Eliza took a deep breath to steady her voice. "I know what you said at the inquest, but now we have more information, it doesn't make sense. For Mrs Milwood to die when she did, somebody must have given her the digitalis in the middle of the night. That raises two problems. One. How could anyone do that while she was asleep without waking the rest of the house, and two, why did it take so long for her to be sick?"

"Perhaps she wasn't asleep." Archie raised an eyebrow at her. "If someone knew she had difficulty sleeping they may have given her a sleeping draught laced with the poison?"

Eliza thought for a moment. "I checked the medicine cabinet and there wasn't anything to suggest she had trouble sleeping. We've had the results back for the tonic wine and there wasn't anything unusual in that; the only other thing was the herbal medicine. If insomnia was a recurring problem, you'd think she'd have taken something for it."

"Why didn't you bring the herbal medicine for testing too?"

Eliza shrugged. "There didn't seem much point. Judith said she hadn't taken any recently and the bottle was almost full. Even if it contained digitalis, she hadn't taken enough for it to do her any harm."

"Not if it was the original recipe, but what if someone had tampered with it and added dried leaves to the mixture after they'd used it?"

Eliza banged a hand on her forehead. "Why didn't I think of that? It's more likely to be the culprit than the tonic wine."

"Not necessarily. It would have taken some planning, but it's a possibility."

"Would it have helped her sleep though?" Connie asked.

"No, you're right," Archie said. "The police might be better looking for a missing bottle of morphine or something similar. If she had difficulty sleeping, that would be a more obvious choice. The murderer could have taken it with them to throw us off the scent."

"You're right." Eliza put a hand to her chin as she paced the room. "We're going to the Wilsons' again this afternoon to speak to Flora. While we're there, I'll ask Judith for the herbal medicine and check whether Mrs Milwood took anything to help her sleep."

"Why are you speaking to Flora again?" Archie's brow furrowed.

"We spoke to her yesterday and think she's hiding something from us," Connie said.

Archie turned to speak to Eliza but stopped when there was a knock on the front door.

"Who on earth's this?" Eliza asked. "Can't people see the surgery isn't open in the afternoon?"

Moments later Iris knocked on the dining room door and showed Inspector Adams into the room.

"Dr Thomson, Mrs Thomson, Mrs Appleton." The inspector nodded to them as he stepped into the room. "I hope I'm not disturbing anything."

"No, not at all, it's nice to meet you." Archie stood up and offered his hand to their guest, but Eliza turned her back on them as she gathered her belongings into her bag.

"You've met my wife, I believe." Archie gestured towards Eliza, who forced herself to smile as she turned around.

"Good afternoon, Inspector. If you'll excuse me, I don't want to intrude on gentlemen's business. Shall we go, Connie?"

The inspector held up his hands as if in surrender. "Mrs Thomson, please don't go. I came to apologise for yesterday. I'm sorry if I offended you, I hadn't realised who I was talking to."

"And that makes a difference?"

The inspector glanced at Archie before turning back to his wife. "Sergeant Cooper tells me you're the daughter of Mr Bell."

"What if I am? Do you think it's only acceptable to talk to me in a civilised manner because I have an influential father?"

The inspector coughed to clear his throat. "No, of course not, but now I know who you are, I realise you're a woman of some intelligence. He told me that you've helped more than one police force identify murderers in the past from information you've read in the newspapers."

"And she solved a real-life murder earlier this year." Connie stood firm as she folded her arms in front of her.

"Really? I'm sorry, I didn't know that. I called to say that, with your experience, I'd be delighted if you'd help us."

Eliza glared at him. "Just like that? I thought you'd been sent here to solve the case."

"Eliza!" Archie said.

"It's all right, Dr Thomson. I understand why your wife's angry with me. When we met yesterday I hadn't been fully updated on the details of the investigation. After she left, Sergeant Cooper told me what they'd learned so far." The inspector paused and took a deep breath. "As much as it pains me to say this, that pair at the station couldn't have found out so much if we'd left them another month. In fact, they wouldn't have even thought to ask most of the questions. That suggests these ladies have already been of great assistance."

He studied Eliza, whose expression had not changed. "Please, Mrs Thomson, I've been called back to London and wanted to ask if you'll continue to help the sergeant while I'm gone. Give him an idea of what to look for, if you understand my meaning. I wouldn't mind you keeping that young constable of his in check as well. Will you accept my apology?"

He offered Eliza his hand and after a moment's hesitation she accepted the inspector's handshake. "I will and I'm sure we'll be happy to help as long as you tell the sergeant you've approved our interfering."

"I will, although I wouldn't call it that…"

"And you'll apologise to Sergeant Cooper for talking to him like that in front of us." Connie's voice didn't falter. "If you had any issues with him, you should have waited until we'd gone."

The inspector offered Connie his hand. "Yes, of course. I

hope you'll accept my apology as well. I meant no offence, it was just ... well, it doesn't matter."

"You thought that investigating a murder was no job for two women. Am I right?" Eliza's face remained stern.

The inspector's face reddened.

"Unfortunately, you're not the first man I've met who thinks that and I don't suppose you'll be the last."

The inspector shrugged. "It's just that it's not usual..."

"Inspector, please don't use the word *usual* in any sentence that refers to my wife." Archie gave Eliza a sideways glance. "If you ever get to know her, you'll realise she's quite unique, and has a very loyal friend."

Inspector Adams finally smiled. "I swear I won't make that mistake again, I've learned my lesson."

"I'm glad to hear it." The sparkle returned to Eliza's eyes. "Now, I suggest we say no more about it and get on with finding this murderer. If we learn anything of particular interest shall I write to you at New Scotland Yard?"

The inspector grimaced. "Let's try to keep everything as official as we can. Tell Sergeant Cooper first and only contact me at New Scotland Yard if you need to. We're at Victoria Embankment..."

"Thank you, I have the address."

"Yes, of course you do. Right, I'll be on my way."

Archie showed the inspector to the front door and as soon as it closed behind him, Eliza beamed at Connie.

"We're back in business. Not only can we go call on Judith and Flora, we have official permission to do so." She clapped her hands together. "Well done for standing up for Sergeant Cooper too."

"Someone had to." Connie's face was stern. "The poor

sergeant didn't know where to look yesterday, he was so embarrassed."

"Well, we'll check he gets his apology. Right now, are we ready to go?"

"Not so fast." Archie walked back into the room as Eliza picked up her bag. "Just because the inspector has asked for help, doesn't mean you're now leading the investigation."

Eliza grinned. "What on earth makes you think I'd do that?"

CHAPTER FOURTEEN

L ess than five minutes later, Eliza and Connie made their way across the village green towards the Wilsons' house. No sooner had they arrived than Judith opened the door to them.

"My, here again, how lovely. Is it a social call or are you here to ask more questions?"

"A bit of both," Eliza said.

"We're always happy to make a social visit and you're more than welcome to come over to our side of the village," Connie said. "You should at least find someone in one of the houses, unless one of us takes the long way round and the other cuts across the green."

Judith laughed. "We need to agree on which way round we should walk then. Let me get us some tea."

"While you do that, would you mind if I ask you a few questions?" Eliza said.

"No, of course not, come with me." Judith led the way to the kitchen. "How can I help this time?"

Eliza's brow creased. "There's something about the timing

of Mrs Milwood's death that doesn't feel right and I wondered if she was a good sleeper. Did she ever take anything to help her sleep?"

Judith's brow furrowed. "Now you mention it, I've got a feeling that might have been the reason the doctor prescribed the herbal medicine. She had a lot of trouble dropping off these last few months."

"But she didn't take it?"

"No. I don't know what was in it, but she complained it didn't work and gave up on it. You can see the bottle's hardly been touched."

"And this was the first bottle she'd had?"

Judith nodded as she put the kettle onto the stove. "Yes, I think so."

"Did she try anything else?"

"Nothing from the doctor. More recently she'd taken to having a brandy about half an hour before bedtime. She said it did the job better than any medicines and so she had one most evenings."

Eliza cocked her head to one side. "Did she have one the night before she died?"

"She did..." Judith put her hand to her mouth as her eyes widened "...and I forgot to tell you."

Eliza took a breath. "Who poured it for her?"

"I did."

"Did anyone see you?"

Judith sighed. "Not pouring the brandy, because we keep it in the dining room, but I had to go to the kitchen to get it topped up with a bit of water; it was too strong for her on its own. Cook had a jug of water on one of the dressers near the cooking range and she put a dash into the glass."

"And no one else touched it?"

"Not that I'm aware of. Do you think it's important?"

"I can't be sure." Eliza paced the kitchen while she recapped the information. "Did she usually take the glass to bed with her?"

"No, not usually. She'd drink it in the drawing room before going to bed, and I'd take it back to the kitchen when I went to get her some water."

"And you did that the night before she died?"

Judith took the boiling kettle from the stove. "I would have done, I did it every night."

"Did Mrs Harris see you get the water?"

"No, she wasn't there by that time. She's always up early to get the bread rising and so she goes up to her room as soon as she's tidied up after dinner."

Eliza sighed. "All right, thank you."

Judith poured the water into the teapot and set it on the tray. "If you're done with your questions, shall we go into the drawing room?"

"That would be lovely," Connie said. "Especially if there's any more of that nice cake."

"Let me see what I've got." Judith headed towards the pantry.

"While we're here, do you mind if I help myself to that bottle of herbal medicine in the cabinet? I'd like to take it back to the surgery," Eliza asked. "I don't suppose there's much wrong with it, but we should check everything to be on the safe side."

Judith shrugged. "Take what you like."

"Actually, while the tea's brewing, could we have a quick word with Flora? Is she in?"

"Flora? How can she help?"

Eliza sighed. "To tell you the truth, I'm not sure, but we need to speak to everyone and so if you wouldn't mind showing us the way. I'm sure we'll be back by the time the tea's ready."

Judith's gaze rested on Eliza before she nodded. "You'd better follow me."

They reached the top floor to find three closed doors. Judith knocked on the one to the left.

"Flora darling, you have visitors. Can we come in?"

Eliza stiffened as a bolt was pulled back across the door; a moment later it opened to reveal Flora standing in front of them.

"Oh, it's you."

Eliza put on her best smile. "May we come in? We have a couple of questions for you."

"I suppose so."

Eliza scanned the room while she waited for Judith to leave them. "Why did you lie to us yesterday, Flora?"

Flora took a step backwards, her eyes wide. "I didn't."

"I saw you outside the surgery," Connie said. "Mrs Petty saw you too. Why won't you tell us what you were doing there?"

Flora fidgeted with her fingers and took a deep breath. "All I was doing was going to the shop but when I was nearly there, I realised I'd forgotten my money and so I turned back."

Eliza studied the girl in front of her. "The most direct route from here to the shop doesn't take you past the surgery."

"No." Flora didn't meet Eliza's gaze. "I was embarrassed that I had to turn around in the middle of the street and so tried to make it look deliberate by walking back past the pond."

"And that was all there was to it?" Connie asked.

Flora nodded.

"Then why lie about it?" Eliza crossed the room to the window as she waited for an answer.

"I don't know. I didn't want to appear foolish, I suppose."

"And so what about Sam? What was he doing there?"

Flora glanced at Connie.

"Yes, Mrs Appleton saw him there too." Eliza turned back from the window to stare at Connie, willing her to say nothing.

"All right, yes, I did see him, but I don't know what he was doing. When I asked him he told me to mind my own business and so I came home."

"Across the green and not around the pond," Connie said as a point of fact rather than a question.

"Yes. I was cross because he wouldn't tell me, and so I went off the idea of going for a walk."

"Thank you," Eliza said. "It would have been much easier if you'd told us the truth first time around, although I suspect there's still something you're not telling us. We'll leave it at that for today, but I want you to think carefully about what you've told us and who you're trying to protect. At the moment the police consider your mother to be the prime suspect in this murder case. We're trying to clear her name and if you want to help her, you'd better tell us what you know."

CHAPTER FIFTEEN

With a final farewell to Judith, Eliza and Connie made their way to the police station.

"I hope the inspector told Sergeant Cooper he's allowed to talk to us again," Connie said.

"Well, if he hasn't, we will." Eliza grinned at her friend.

"What will we tell him? That Sam and Flora were at the surgery last Monday afternoon?"

"Yes, although I'm not sure how it helps us."

Connie stared at Eliza. "Well, it shows Flora lied to us for one thing. And why wasn't Sam at work when he should have been?"

"You're right, of course, but what does it tell us? That they were up to no good or that they were in the wrong place at the wrong time? We've no evidence they were doing anything they shouldn't have been."

"Then why lie about it?" Connie couldn't keep the exasperation from her voice.

"Sam hasn't lied to us. We haven't even spoken to him, something we must rectify tomorrow, Frank as well, but ...

well, I can understand Flora. She's a bright girl who wants to make something of herself and yet she felt silly forgetting her money. I can understand she wouldn't want us to think badly of her."

"I'm sure everyone's forgotten something at some time in their lives. I know I have."

"My dear Connie, I fear you forget what it's like to be young. They aren't able to dismiss things as easily as we can."

Connie nodded. "Maybe you're right, although how do we know she's telling the truth? She may have said she'd forgotten her money, but she hadn't intended to go to the shop in the first place, or she had the money, but was up to something else as well."

"That had crossed my mind. As I told her, we'll speak to her again, but for now let's give her some time to ponder her mother's position. It may make her more willing to talk to us. In the meantime, shall we see what Sergeant Cooper has for us?"

The sergeant was behind the desk as they walked into the police station and as soon as he looked up he gave them a broad smile.

"Good afternoon, ladies, I hoped you'd be back after the little 'misunderstanding' with Inspector Adams. These London lads think they're the only ones with brains."

Connie frowned. "I hope he apologised to you."

"He did indeed, Mrs Appleton, all thanks to you, I believe."

Connie's cheeks coloured, and she lowered her eyes as the sergeant gazed at her.

Eliza struggled to suppress a smile. "Do you have anything for us this afternoon, Sergeant Cooper?" she asked.

The sergeant flinched at the sound of his name. "Oh yes, where are my manners? Come into the back room and take a seat. Jenkins can take over here. I've something to tell you."

Constable Jenkins glared at his boss as he ushered him towards the desk.

"Fancies himself as a detective, he does." The sergeant nodded after Jenkins. "Thinks he's above desk duty, but we've all got to do it."

"Quite." Eliza gave the constable a pointed look before moving to the back room. "What was it you had to tell us? Did you speak to Mr Hewitt?"

"No, he wasn't at the church when we called this morning and so I took Jenkins with me to Over Moreton to check Mr Wilson's alibi. You'll never guess what. He wasn't in work on the afternoon of the murder."

"Wasn't in work?" Connie's eyes widened as she turned to Eliza.

Eliza stared at the sergeant. "You spoke to him this morning? Was he the one who told you?"

"We spoke to him but it was his boss who mentioned he'd been off work that day. Mr Wilson initially denied it but later said he'd mixed up his dates."

"What nonsense." Eliza stood up to pace the floor. "You don't forget what you did hours before you find your mother dead. Did he say where he was?"

Sergeant Cooper took a deep breath. "He said it was personal business."

"And you didn't remind him that this is a murder inquiry? What is he up to ... and why didn't Judith tell us? We've spoken to her often enough and on every occasion she said he was at work."

Connie's face paled. "Maybe she didn't know."

Eliza stopped where she was. "Or perhaps she didn't want us finding out. She may be telling the truth when she says she didn't murder Mrs Milwood, but that doesn't mean she doesn't know who did."

"You can't really think that." Connie turned to the sergeant, whose eyes were fixed on Eliza. "You don't agree with her, do you, Sergeant?"

Sergeant Cooper's eyes flicked to Connie. "I think Mrs Thomson has a point, but at the moment my money's on Samuel Wilson."

"Sam? Why? What have you found out about him?" Eliza said.

"That's what I'm coming to. While we were in Over Moreton we planned on talking to him, as we discussed it the other day, but it turns out he wasn't in work that day either, and..." he paused to make sure he had their full attention "... he's gone missing. Nobody's seen him since the day of the murder."

"Sam's gone missing?" Connie put her hands to her cheeks.

The sergeant nodded with a self-satisfied grin on his face.

"Were they all in it together?" Eliza's voice was a whisper. "Each one providing an alibi for the other?"

Constable Jenkins popped his head round the door. "If you want my opinion, Mr Wilson and his son should both be arrested immediately. I don't think the mother's involved, but they've clearly planned this together."

Eliza's head jolted towards Constable Jenkins. "No, don't arrest them. It's not a crime to take time off work, or even to leave Over Moreton. We'll need more evidence before you can charge them and it would be more helpful if they weren't behind bars, for the time being at least." She turned to Sergeant Cooper for confirmation he'd heard. "You understand, Sergeant?" When he nodded his agreement, Constable Jenkins glared first at Eliza and then at the sergeant before retreating to the desk.

"Sergeant, please give us time to speak to Mr Wilson, and Sam if we can find him. Did you look for Sam in the room he lodges in?"

The sergeant's posture slumped. "No, we didn't. Mr Royal said he hadn't been in work all week and had left no word of where he'd gone and so..."

"And so you assumed he'd left Over Moreton? What if he's ill? He might be laid up in bed with no one to explain his absence to work."

When the sergeant continued to stare at his desk, Eliza returned to the seat opposite him. "It's too late for us to travel to Over Moreton now, but Mrs Appleton and I will pay Mr Wilson a visit tonight and then we'll see if we can find Sam tomorrow."

Despite the early evening sun Eliza shivered as she and Connie left the police station.

"Do you really think Sam's ill?" Connie asked.

Eliza sighed. "It's possible, although I'll admit it's not probable. I agree with the police that something isn't right, but I don't want him arrested before we've had the chance to talk to him. There could be any number of reasons for his disappearance."

Connie nodded before glancing at Eliza. "Such as?"

"I don't know, but we can't assume he's guilty before we talk to him. Now, I suggest we both go home and get something to eat and then we'll pay a visit to Judith and Mr Wilson."

"She'll be tired of us calling all the time."

"I'm afraid that can't be avoided. We're trying to help her."

Connie suddenly stopped. "Do you remember last week we were talking about the murderer and we said that if she didn't poison Mrs Milwood, then someone else must have?"

"And she said the idea scared her!" Eliza's eyes were wide.

Connie nodded. "I wonder if she's had her suspicions about either Mr Wilson or Sam."

"Oh my goodness, I hope not. We're supposed to be helping her, but the more we learn, the worse it looks. Why didn't she tell us about Mr Wilson?"

"Do you think she deliberately didn't tell us?"

"At the moment, I don't know what to think." Eliza stopped as they arrived outside the surgery. "I need to decide how to approach this. Meet me here in an hour and we'll see what they've got to say for themselves."

CHAPTER SIXTEEN

The sun was still pleasant as they walked across the green, but when Eliza and Connie reached the Wilsons' they had to knock on the door twice before Judith answered.

"Oh, it's you again. I didn't expect you to call at this hour." Judith spoke through the partially opened front door.

"No, I'm sorry, but we need to speak to Mr Wilson and we wanted to be sure he was home from work. May we come in?"

Judith's face was stern. "Must you? He's had a difficult day."

Eliza took a deep breath. "Yes, we're aware of that, that's why we'd like to speak to him. Have you forgotten we're trying to help you?"

Judith hesitated before opening the door fully. "I'm sorry, it's just that with you working with the police now ... it doesn't seem right."

Eliza and Connie remained silent as they followed Judith into the drawing room where Mr Wilson sat by the fireplace, his head in his hands.

"Mrs Thomson and Mrs Appleton to see you." Judith followed them into the room and closed the door behind her.

"Ladies ... g-good evening..." Mr Wilson sprang to his feet. "To what do we owe the pleasure?"

Eliza didn't wait to be asked to sit down. "We're trying to help you, but we can't do that if we don't speak to you. We heard from Sergeant Cooper earlier that he came to see you in work."

"Yes."

"Mr Royal told them you hadn't been in work on the afternoon of your mother's death. Something you failed to mention. When they reminded you, you said you'd got your dates mixed up. Does that mean you don't have an alibi?"

"I do have an alibi." Mr Wilson's voice was an octave higher than usual.

Eliza raised an eyebrow. "Would you care to share it with us?"

Mr Wilson drained the whisky from the glass that stood on the table beside his chair. When he failed to respond, Eliza continued. "Mr Wilson, I'm not sure you realise, but you're in a very precarious position at the moment. Unless we can give the police a good reason for your absence from work, I fear that by this time tomorrow you could be under arrest."

"Arrest!" Judith glowered at Eliza. "They can't do that."

"Judith, be quiet," Mr Wilson snapped at his wife. "She's exaggerating."

Eliza studied Judith and Mr Wilson, who now sat side by side on the settee. "I'm afraid I'm not. Judith, when you asked for help, I believed you had nothing to do with Mrs Milwood's death and that in return for our help you'd tell us the truth in all matters. How can I help you if the police keep finding new pieces of evidence you haven't told me about? If you knew Mr Wilson wasn't in work on the afternoon in question, why on earth didn't you tell us ... especially if he had another alibi?"

Judith stared at her husband.

"Because she didn't know." Mr Wilson mumbled his words.

Tears formed in Judith's eyes. "I didn't, not until this evening."

"Perhaps you'd better tell us what happened then, Mr Wilson."

Mr Wilson kept his eyes fixed on the carpet. "I went into work as usual that morning, but we were quiet and so I asked if I could take the afternoon off. I wanted to go into London to see someone."

"And did you? See someone, that is."

Mr Wilson nodded. "I did."

"You'll need to provide me with their name and address so the police can confirm it. Not that it will help in the long run, because as you've heard, whoever gave your mother the poison did so long before that afternoon."

"Well, if it makes no difference..."

"Oh, it makes a difference, Mr Wilson, a difference between whether you spend tomorrow night in a police cell or here at home. The police are keen to show their worth by arresting someone before the inspector comes back from London, and at the moment, your name is very near the top of their list."

Mr Wilson sighed. "If you must know, I went to London to ask if I could get my old job back at Moreton Industries."

"The job you had before you came to live with Mrs Milwood?"

Mr Wilson nodded.

"So you planned on moving back to London despite it being against your mother's wishes?"

Mr Wilson pushed himself up and walked to the sideboard to pour another whisky. "We couldn't stay here any longer. She was destroying the family by turning us against each other. I thought that if we got away..." He took a large mouthful of the amber liquid.

"Couldn't you have written to Moreton Industries?" Connie asked. "Did you need to go all the way to London?"

"It wasn't that simple." He sat back in his chair. "They offered me my job back last month but within a week of receiving the offer, they withdrew it. I wanted to ask them why."

"And did you find out?"

"No. All they'd say was that they'd had an objection to my returning; they wouldn't tell me who from or why."

"And you knew nothing of this?" Eliza stared at Judith, but she averted her gaze.

"No."

"And is that the same reason you didn't tell us that Sam's missing?"

Judith's hands flew to her mouth.

"Yes, we know about that too. When the police spoke to Mr Wilson, they were looking for Sam as well. Apparently nobody's seen him since the day of Mrs Milwood's death." Eliza's gaze hardened. "You work with him, Mr Wilson. I won't believe you didn't know he was missing, or that you didn't tell Judith. Why on earth didn't one of you tell us?"

Judith took her handkerchief from her pocket and wiped her eyes. "We don't know where he is."

Eliza looked between husband and wife. "Do you realise that by disappearing like that, without a word to anyone, he's put himself right at the top of the police's list of suspects? If Constable Jenkins has his way, he'll have Sam locked up as soon as he sees him and will ask questions later. When did you last see him?"

Judith sobbed into her handkerchief. "I haven't seen him since he left home, four weeks on Monday."

"But Mr Wilson must have."

Mr Wilson sighed. "He was in work on the morning of Mother's death. I told him I was going to London, I thought someone should know, but that was the last time I saw him."

"So Sam knew you'd be in London that afternoon?"

Mr Wilson eyed Eliza. "What do you mean?"

"According to the police, Sam left work shortly after you did and they think he came here."

"And I wasn't here for him," Judith wailed through her tears.

Mr Wilson shifted in his seat.

"Is there something else you want to tell us, Mr Wilson?" Eliza asked.

After taking another gulp of his drink he stood up and walked to the window. "We think we had a burglary on the afternoon of the murder."

Eliza looked to Connie before staring at Mr Wilson. "And you didn't report it?"

He shook his head.

"What did they take?"

"Some money."

Eliza's eyes narrowed to slits. "How much money?"

Mr Wilson shrugged. "I can't say for certain because

Mother would use the money in the safe if she ever needed to, but I'd say over one hundred pounds."

Eliza's mouth opened and closed several times before she found the right words. "Let me get this straight. You're telling me that someone walked into the house, opened the safe and walked out again with over one hundred pounds?"

Mr Wilson nodded his head.

"Did they close the safe again?" Connie waited for a reply, but a moment later, all eyes were on her. "Don't look at me like that, it's a perfectly reasonable question. How many burglars lock the safe after them?"

"That's a good point," Eliza said as she turned back to Mr Wilson. When he remained silent, she continued. "They did, didn't they? That's why you were uncertain the theft even took place, and why you didn't report it straight away. When did you notice the money was missing?"

"On the Friday morning, Judith needed to go to the shop and so I went to the safe to get her some money. The problem was, there wasn't as much in there as I'd expected."

"And why do you think the theft took place on the Wednesday?"

"Because I'd taken some money out on Tuesday and then because of Mother's *incident*, we were all here on Thursday. It must have gone missing on the Wednesday when we were both out."

Eliza nodded. "Where was Flora while all this was going on?"

"She never hears a thing in that attic," Mr Wilson said. "The place could be ransacked and she wouldn't notice until it was too late."

Eliza paused and studied the Wilsons. "Judging by your

reactions and given that the money was taken from the safe ... which was then locked again ... I would say you're afraid Sam took the money. Am I right?"

Judith's sobs grew louder. "What if he did and someone saw him? They can't send him to the gallows."

Connie sighed. "It doesn't look good, does it?"

"On the face of it, no it doesn't," Eliza said, "but as I keep telling people, Mrs Milwood was poisoned up to twelve hours before she died. If Sam only called here that afternoon, he may have taken the money, but I doubt he's the killer."

"What if he was the one who called earlier in the day and unlocked the front door?" Connie asked.

"That would certainly change things." Eliza sighed. "We need to see if we can find him and ask him exactly what he was doing in the hours before Mrs Milwood was murdered."

Judith wiped her eyes and nose. "Eliza, please don't tell the police about the money. We can't be certain it was Sam, but if it was, we don't want him getting into trouble for it. It was family money anyway. If you see him, will you ask him to come home? Tell him we're not angry about it."

"You might not be..." Mr Wilson started, but stopped at the look on his wife's face. "Very well. Just tell him we want to know he's safe and that Judith would like to see him. Please ask him to come home ... at least for a cup of tea."

CHAPTER SEVENTEEN

When Eliza awoke the next day, she was relieved to remember it was Saturday and there was no morning surgery. Despite that it would be a busy morning if they wanted to get to Over Moreton and speak to Sam before the workshop closed. She dressed quickly in a navy skirt with matching jacket and went downstairs for breakfast. Archie followed her into the dining room two minutes later.

"You're looking very formal for a Saturday. Have you forgotten there's no surgery?"

"No, not at all." She waited for Iris to place a dish of kedgeree on the table and disappear back to the kitchen. "We need to find Sam, Judith's eldest son. Nobody's seen him since the day Mrs Milwood died and Mr Wilson thinks he took a large sum of money from them. They're desperate to know he's safe and we need to establish where he's been before the police find him."

"You're not interfering again, are you? If the police want to find him, shouldn't you let them?"

"No, not at all." She took a mouthful of the smoked

haddock. "All the police know is that he disappeared on the day of the murder and as far as they're concerned that's enough reason to arrest him. They're oblivious to the fact that the murderer administered the poison hours before Mrs Milwood died."

"I don't like this, Eliza." Archie put down his knife and fork and gazed at his wife. "What if he is the murderer? If you go asking too many questions, he may turn nasty."

"Don't be silly. He's a young boy, only about the same age as Henry. I'm not going to accuse him of anything. I want to help. Why would he hurt me?"

"Because young men have a habit of lashing out if they feel trapped."

Eliza grimaced. "I know you worry, but there's really no need. Besides, Connie will be with me, it'll be two against one."

Archie shook his head. "Promise me you'll only look for him in places where there are other people. Don't go walking into the fields where he could find you on your own."

"What do you take me for? I'm going to Over Moreton, to Royal's workshop where Sam works, and maybe to the boarding house where he rents a room. When did you ever see me walking through fields?"

The corners of Archie's mouth finally turned into a smile. "I'm sure you must have done ... once. All right, but be careful and be back here in time for luncheon."

Fifteen minutes later, Eliza stood outside Connie's front door and gave a hearty rap on the door-knocker. "Are you all set?" she asked as Connie opened her front door.

"I am. Are we walking or do you have the carriage?"

Eliza eyed her friend. "Not you too. You're the second

person today to suggest I plan on walking further than the village shop. No, don't be silly. Archie's asked the stable boy to get the carriage ready for us."

"Jolly good, I was hoping you'd say that. Shall we walk up to the police station first to check they've not spoken to Sam already?"

"No, I'd rather not. Even if they've spoken to him, they won't have asked the right questions. We're better off doing it ourselves. Especially after what we learned last night."

"What if they've found him already and arrested him? We'll be wasting our time."

Eliza sighed. "It's a chance we'll have to take. If you ask me, the only way they'll have found him is if Sam turned up at the police station and handed himself in. I doubt that's happened."

"No, but I wouldn't trust Constable Jenkins to ask questions first," Connie said.

"I wouldn't either, but let's hope we find him before they do. Ah, here's the carriage now. Let's get a move on, it seems we have no time to lose."

The village of Over Moreton was bigger than Moreton-on-Thames and ten minutes later Eliza guided the carriage along the main shopping street to a spot at the far end, directly outside the workshop of Royal & Sons. She climbed down and manoeuvred the horses to a water trough.

"We might as well start here, given that this is where he's supposed to be."

She helped Connie out of the carriage and shuddered as she inspected the outside of the single-storey red-brick building. "I don't know about anything else, but it could do with a good clean. Are you ready?"

Connie's nod was less than convincing but Eliza took a deep breath and they walked through the door into a cavernous room with a large furnace to one side and a multitude of men working around it. As they stood by the door the noise in the factory reduced until all the men were staring at them.

Eliza straightened her back before striding into the room. "Good morning, gentlemen. Could you tell me who's in charge here?"

"That would be me, luv." An elderly man with a balding head and a face smeared with soot walked towards her. "What can I do for yer?"

Eliza shuddered as he ran his eyes over her. "I'd like to speak to Mr Royal if possible. Is he here?"

"Good morning, ladies." Eliza turned to her left where a young man of above average height and dark brown hair stood in a doorway. "I'm Mr Royal, please come this way." He gestured for them to join him in his office and closed the door behind them. "Please forgive the men, it isn't often we have female company around here. How can I help you?"

Eliza flushed. "Excuse me, but I was expecting someone much older."

Mr Royal flashed a warm smile. "That would be my father, he's all but retired now."

"Of course, I should have realised, but not to worry. I'm Mrs Thomson and this is my friend Mrs Appleton. We're helping the police in Moreton-on-Thames with their enquiries into the death of a resident. She's the grandmother of one of your clerks, Samuel Wilson. Is he in work today?"

Mr Royal pursed his lips, sucking air through them as he did. "You're not the first people who've wanted a word with young Mr Wilson. We had the police here yesterday. I'll tell you what I told them. He left here around midday on Wednesday last week and we haven't seen him since."

Eliza nodded. "I'll take that as a no then. Has anyone been to his room to inquire after his health?"

"His health?" Mr Royal's brow creased.

"Well, yes. Is it so incredible to think the boy may be ill? He lives on his own in a room in the village. If he were ill, he wouldn't be able to get word to you."

"If he was ill enough to be off for over a week, I'm sure his landlady could come and tell us."

"Really?" Eliza said. "And walk into an environment like this? With all due respect, it's no place for a woman even if she is only delivering a message."

Mr Royal bristled. "Well, he could have written. There's a letter box in the door, someone could have posted it through."

"We can't assume that. Do you happen to have his address? I'd like to pay his landlady a visit in case he is confined to bed."

Mr Royal nodded and turned to a pile of folders on his desk. "Here we are." He pulled a sheet of paper from the stack and copied the address out for them.

"Would you be able to direct us?" Eliza asked as he handed over the paper.

"It's on the other side of the village, near the road to Moreton-on-Thames. Turn left out of here and go to the far end of the village before turning left again. It's about the tenth house down."

"Thank you, Mr Royal, you've been most helpful."

As soon as they were away from the workshop, Eliza followed Connie back into the carriage and let out a sigh.

"What a dreadful place to work. You can't blame the Wilsons for wanting to go back to London."

Connie nodded. "You're right and you're right about no woman wanting to go in there. I wouldn't have gone in without you."

"I should hope not, looking as glamorous as you do today. You wouldn't have stood a chance." Eliza admired her friend's silver-grey skirt and navy blouse. "Now, let's be going and hope that Sam's at home."

The main street was busy and Eliza manoeuvred the carriage to the far end. As they approached the turning for Sam's lodgings, she pulled in to the side of the road.

"We can walk from here, it shouldn't be far."

With the horses tethered, they strolled down the road looking for the house that matched the address on the paper. It was a street lined with two-storey terraced houses, and once they'd found the one they were looking for, Eliza knocked on the door before stepping back to study the exterior. Moments later, a short, plump woman wearing a colourful apron answered the door.

"Yes?"

Eliza flashed her most endearing smile. "Good afternoon. Could you tell me, is this the house where Samuel Wilson keeps a room?"

The woman glared at her. "What's it to you?"

"We're friends of his mother and wondered if we might have a quick word with him."

"He ain't here."

"Oh, what a shame," Connie said. "Mrs Wilson will be upset."

Eliza nodded. "She will. Did he say when he'd be back?"

The woman shrugged. "He's not been here for over a week. He paid me a month's rent in advance last Tuesday evening as I was going to bed."

"He did?" Eliza's smile gained a response from the landlady and her face softened. "What time would that have been?"

"I always lock the front door at ten and go straight upstairs. It was just before then."

"Could he have gone out once you'd locked up?"

"Not unless he shinned down the drainpipe. There's only one key and I keep it with me." She pulled on a chain around her neck to reveal the key.

Eliza nodded. "And did you see him again after that?"

"He went to his room as I was locking up and was down at breakfast for half past seven the next morning. I assumed he'd gone to work as usual, but he didn't come back for his dinner that night and I've not seen him since."

"Why would he pay for a month's rent and then disappear?" Connie asked.

The landlady shrugged. "I'm beggared if I know, but he left all his things and so I'm expecting him back before the month's up."

"That's marvellous." Connie's eyes lit up. "Did he say where he was going?"

The woman folded her arms across her ample bosom. "Didn't say, and I didn't ask. I let my lodgers keep themselves to themselves. Ask no questions, get no lies."

"Quite." Eliza strained to see into the house over the woman's shoulder. "Would there be anyone else here he might have spoken to?"

"None that's here now."

"But there was someone?" Eliza's eyes darted back to the woman.

"Not that lived here, but he had a lady friend who worked up at the manor house. She might know."

"He had a young lady?" Eliza beamed at Connie. "You wouldn't happen to have her name, would you?"

The woman's forehead creased. "He mentioned it once, but I forget now. Not one of your common-or-garden names."

"Oh, that's a shame, I expect a lot of young girls work up at the manor house. I wonder how he met her."

The landlady finally smiled. "That I can tell you. He said she used to be a maid at his grandmother's house but moved to Over Moreton when this job became available."

"Ruby!" Connie squealed.

"Yes, that was it. Do you know her?"

"We know of her, but I've never met her," Eliza said truthfully. "Could you direct us to the manor house?"

"It's quite a walk. I doubt you'll get there and back in less than an hour."

Eliza glanced down at her straight skirt. *Do I really look dressed for walking?* "Don't worry about us. We have a carriage at the end of the street, and so if you could point us in the right direction, I'm sure we'll find it."

CHAPTER EIGHTEEN

W ishing Sam's landlady farewell, Eliza and Connie made their way back to the carriage.

"Well, well," Eliza said. "Who'd have thought Sam and Ruby were walking out together? I'm sure Judith knows nothing about it. I bet the police don't either."

"Do you think that's why he left home?" Connie asked. "To be closer to her? It would be rather a trek to travel here from Moreton-on-Thames if he wanted to walk out with her."

"That, my dear, is what we need to find out. Do you know the girl at all?"

"Not really. I've said good morning to her once or twice, but nothing more."

"Well, let's get a move on then and see what we can find out."

The morning air was positively warm by the time they arrived at the manor house, a large, imposing stone-built building, and Eliza was relieved to find it was cooler inside the house than it was outside. The butler gave no hint of curiosity when they asked to speak with Ruby, and without question he showed them into the drawing room.

"If you'll wait here, I'll ask if she's available." He gave a slight bow as he backed out of the room and closed the door.

"My, this takes me back." Eliza strolled around the room, which boasted large floor-to-ceiling windows on two sides, bookshelves on the wall adjacent to the door and an ornate cabinet along the fourth wall. "It's so like our drawing room in the old house in Moreton-on-Thames."

"I don't think I ever went in there," Connie said.

Eliza paused to think. "No, you probably didn't. We were only children and you would have been ushered straight upstairs to play with me in the nursery."

Connie nodded. "You're right, although we did go into the kitchen from time to time, usually when Cook had made a fresh batch of cakes. Do you remember we'd choose the biggest to go with our glass of milk?"

Eliza smiled. "I do. How I loved that house. I don't suppose I'll ever go in again..."

As she spoke the door opened, and the butler escorted Ruby into the room. He introduced them before leaving the three of them alone.

"It's nice to meet you." Eliza smiled at the attractive young girl walking towards them. She wore her dark hair pulled back into a knot at the base of her neck, exaggerating the deep brown eyes set into her round face.

Ruby nodded but said nothing.

"I suppose you're wondering who we are and why we're here."

Ruby again nodded before noticing Connie standing by

the chair opposite Eliza. "I recognise you from Moreton-on-Thames. Are you friendly with Mrs Wilson?"

Connie smiled. "Yes, we are; in fact, she's part of the reason we're here."

"We're looking for her son Sam and understand you're on good terms with him," Eliza said.

Ruby's eyes widened and she took a step backwards. "Who told you that?"

"Don't be alarmed," Eliza said. "We're not here to cause you any trouble. We're here because Mrs Wilson hasn't seen Sam recently and has an urgent need to speak to him. It seems he's disappeared, and we thought you might know where he is."

Ruby bowed her head. "No, I haven't seen him for over a week, since last Tuesday to be precise."

"And you've no idea where he is?"

A tear ran down Ruby's cheek. "He's left me."

"Now, my dear, don't upset yourself." Eliza sat down and patted the cushion beside her. "Come and sit down and tell us about it."

Ruby's head jerked upwards. "Sit down? I can't do that."

"Of course you can, and if anyone says anything they'll have us to answer to. Now, why would Sam go and leave a lovely girl like you?"

"It's all Lord and Lady Harrington-Smyth's fault." Ruby let out a small sob.

"And why would that be?"

Ruby's shoulders sagged. "Last week, His Lordship was having a party and my Wednesday afternoon off was cancelled. It's the only time I get to visit Ma, and Sam would meet me there and walk me home."

"So you couldn't go?" Connie asked.

"No, but I only found out that morning and so I couldn't tell Sam. He must have walked to Moreton-on-Thames to meet me but been angry when I wasn't there."

"I'm sure he wouldn't leave you over something as silly as that," Connie said.

"Well, why else wouldn't he have come to meet me this week? It's the only time we get to be alone. He wouldn't have missed it if he'd been happy with me."

Eliza took Ruby's hand. "Am I right in thinking he moved to Over Moreton to be closer to you?"

Ruby nodded.

"Well then, I'm sure he didn't make that decision lightly. Not seeing you just because you weren't at your ma's makes no sense."

Connie cocked her head to one side. "Can I ask why you moved here in the first place? I imagine it was a lot easier for you to see each other when you worked for his grandmother. Was it the money?"

Ruby's voice was barely audible. "*She* is the reason we're both here."

Eliza quivered at the sudden change in Ruby's tone "What do you mean?"

Ruby shrugged. "I suppose I'd better tell you. Mrs Milwood discovered Sam was fond of me and she was furious."

"Couldn't Sam have spoken to her?"

"He tried, but she told him that unless he stopped seeing me, she'd cut him out of her will."

Connie's eyes narrowed. "The money wouldn't have gone to him, would it? Wouldn't Mr Wilson inherit everything?"

"Oh, you underestimate her. She would have put a clause in the will forbidding Mr Wilson from leaving Sam anything."

"So you did it for Sam, how romantic." Connie's eyes misted over.

"No! We did it for us. We weren't going to let her tell us what to do, but she gave us no option but to move here. She dismissed me from my position with her and arranged a place for me here to make sure I was as far away as possible. She said that if I didn't take the job, I wouldn't get a reference. I had no choice."

"And so despite his grandmother, Sam moved here to be closer to you?"

Ruby nodded. "He told her she could keep her money because what was the point of having it if he couldn't be happy."

"Well, that doesn't sound like the actions of someone who'd walk away from you because you couldn't meet him after work."

Ruby's shoulders slumped. "I suppose not, but I'm worried sick about him."

"Did you know he hasn't been in work all week?"

"I didn't, but that makes it worse…" Ruby sobbed as she searched for her handkerchief.

Eliza waited for her to wipe her eyes. "Is there something else you want to tell us?"

"Only if you're sure you want to help him."

"Yes, of course we do," Connie and Eliza replied together.

"Well, it's just…" Ruby paused.

"Go on."

"I'd seen him at church on the Sunday before he

disappeared and he said he was going to visit Mrs Milwood on the Wednesday to confront her."

"You mean the Wednesday she died?"

Ruby nodded. "The Wednesday I was stuck here."

Eliza's stomach somersaulted. "Oh my goodness."

"He was so angry with her ... and I've been so worried." She buried her face in her hands.

"Oh, my dear." Eliza put her arm around the girl's shoulders. "Do you know what time he planned on going?"

"In the afternoon, he said, but I can't be sure."

Eliza audibly exhaled. "Well, at least that's something. If he did go home, and we can confirm it was in the afternoon, then it's unlikely he could have murdered Mrs Milwood."

Ruby wiped her eyes. "He couldn't have?"

"No, we know she was poisoned, but because of the time she died, she must have been given the drug the night before."

"He wouldn't have gone in the middle of the night. It's too dark to walk down those lanes for one thing. There are no gaslights."

"Yes, of course. Now dry your eyes and Mrs Appleton will go and find us a pot of tea." Eliza's eyes pleaded with Connie, but sensing Ruby was about to object, she held up her hand. "You're our guest and if we want to offer you a cup of tea, I'm sure Her Ladyship won't object." She nodded at Connie, who disappeared from the room to look for the butler.

By the time Connie returned Ruby had dried her eyes and looked more relaxed on the settee.

"Is there anything else you can tell us while we're here?" Eliza asked. "Did Mr or Mrs Wilson know about your friendship with Sam?"

Ruby shrugged. "I can't say for certain but I don't think so.

While I was there, they never said anything to me, but whether Mrs Milwood told them after I left, I've no idea."

"I suspect she didn't. Neither Mr or Mrs Wilson has mentioned it to us." Eliza patted Ruby's hands. "Forgive me for saying this, but you don't sound like a usual domestic servant."

The sadness in Ruby's eyes betrayed her smile. "That's down to my ma. We used to have a bit of money when I was younger. I went to school until I was twelve, but then my dad died. Life wasn't easy after that, but Ma took a job as a maid, and I thought that if she could do it so could I, just until I earn enough to find myself something better."

Eliza smiled. "Mrs Milwood should have been proud of you, not critical. The more I learn about her, the less surprised I am that somebody murdered her."

CHAPTER NINETEEN

The church bells struck one o'clock as Eliza and Connie drove back into Moreton-on-Thames. Eliza flicked the reins of the carriage, causing the horses to break into a trot.

"Good grief, I'll be in trouble. Archie told me to be back in time for luncheon, but he'll have finished by now and mine's likely to be dried up." She turned to face Connie. "Why don't you come in with me for a spot of whatever's left and then he won't be so cross?"

"You make that sound so tempting. Come in for a spot of something dried up and stop Archie shouting at you." Connie smirked at the look on Eliza's face. "It's nice to know I'm useful for something."

"I didn't mean it like that."

"It's a good job for you I've nothing in. I was going to walk to the shop for a bit of ham."

"Well, that suits both of us then! I'll take the carriage around the back and tell him I needed to attend to the horses. That will explain some of our lateness."

By the time they arrived in the dining room, Archie was nowhere to be seen and Eliza breathed a sigh of relief.

"So, what do you have planned for this afternoon?" Connie asked as Iris served them each a bowl of soup.

Eliza's shoulders slumped. "As much as I don't want to, I think we need to speak to Sergeant Cooper."

"That's not such a bad thing," Connie said. "Will you tell him what we've learned about Sam?"

"Not if I can help it. I'd rather hear what they've been up to. I'm still nervous that they'll do something hasty. In some ways I wish the inspector would come back so he can order them not to lock up half the suspects."

"I doubt he'll come on a Saturday."

"No, you're right, but let's go and find out what they're up to. I want to post a couple of letters on the way too."

The walk to the post office only took five minutes and as the letters fluttered down into the postbox, Connie was nearly knocked over by Mr Hewitt leaving the shop next door.

"My dear Mrs Appleton, I'm so sorry. I really should watch where I'm going." Mr Hewitt's high-pitched nasal tone cut through the air.

"No harm done," Connie said. "You must be in a hurry, please go on ahead of us."

"I'm not in such a hurry that I can't remember my manners. Please, let me escort you ... as far as the church at least."

The church bells struck two o'clock as the three of them left the shop.

"We haven't been properly introduced." Mr Hewitt gestured towards Eliza.

"I'm so sorry, my manners have clearly left me, too,"

Connie said. "Mr Hewitt, this is Mrs Thomson, Dr Thomson's wife; Eliza, this is Mr Hewitt the churchwarden."

Eliza nodded at their companion. "You probably won't thank me for saying this, but I remember you from my time at Sunday school."

Mr Hewitt's face creased as he studied her.

"You may remember me as Eliza Bell?"

"Good gracious, yes I do. How long ago is it since you left?"

Eliza smiled. "Nearly thirty years."

"And your father's still well?"

"He is, thank you. He's supposed to be retired, but he can't help involving himself in everything around him."

Mr Hewitt nodded. "He's not changed then. Well, send him my regards. Maybe he'll come back to Moreton himself now you're here."

"I'm sure he will. I must invite him to stay so he can meet everyone again."

They stopped by the church gates and Eliza glanced up at the bell tower, which was now directly in front of them.

"Mrs Appleton tells me you're having trouble with the bell tower."

"Sadly, we are. The stonework's crumbling and the rain manages to find its way into every nook and cranny; it was coming in as fast as we could mop it up last Sunday."

"Yes, I saw you with the buckets out. Perhaps we need to start asking for donations."

"We started collecting several weeks ago and reached our goal within a week when someone pledged a rather sizeable donation."

Connie clapped her hands beneath her chin. "How marvellous. Why didn't you announce it?"

"Unfortunately, we were asked to keep the donation quiet and so we couldn't. In many ways, it was for the best as we're no longer sure we'll be getting the money."

"What a shame." Connie's posture slumped. "Why would someone suddenly change their mind about a donation?"

"It wasn't as simple as that." Mr Hewitt gazed up at the building. "Are you ladies in a hurry or will you walk into church with me? I need to get these to the vicar." He held up a brown paper parcel. "The reason for my haste earlier and so I'd better not be late."

Eliza nodded and the three of them walked up the path to the church. "Are you at liberty to tell us why the donation was withdrawn?"

"It's difficult at the moment because we can't say for certain that we won't be getting the money. Shall we just say the benefactor's no longer with us?"

Eliza stopped by the church door and glanced at Connie before she spoke. "It wouldn't have anything to do with the death of Mrs Milwood, would it?"

Mr Hewitt hesitated. "I've probably said too much already, but as you ask, yes it would."

"Please, Mr Hewitt, don't go in," Eliza said. "This may seem irregular, but would you be able to give us a few details? We're officially working with the police to discover Mrs Milwood's killer and you may have some information that could help. We were going to call and see you at some point, anyway."

"The police?" Mr Hewitt gave a nervous glance at the church door. "I'm sure I don't know anything."

"We only want to ask you a few questions. Several witnesses have told us you called on Mrs Milwood on the Tuesday before she died. Can you tell us what time that would have been?"

Mr Hewitt cleared his throat. "If I remember correctly, the bells had sounded for half past four when I left here. I didn't stay long, maybe a quarter of an hour."

"Can you tell us why you called?"

Mr Hewitt peered over his shoulder. "The information was given in confidence and so I'd be obliged if it didn't go any further."

"You have our word." Connie nodded as Eliza spoke.

Mr Hewitt lowered his voice. "I received a letter from Mrs Milwood on what turned out to be the morning before she died asking me to call at the house later that day. As you're aware, I did."

"And this is where she offered you the donation?"

Mr Hewitt ran a finger around his collar. "Not exactly. She'd already mentioned it several weeks earlier, but given the urgency of the repairs I'd written to ask when we might receive the money. When I called, I was hoping for an answer."

"And did you get one?"

"In a manner of speaking." He took a deep breath. "She told me she was leaving the donation in her Last Will and Testament."

Eliza's mouth dropped open as Mr Hewitt kicked at some loose stones.

"Oh my goodness," Connie said.

"Quite." Eliza rubbed her forehead. "Forgive me for being

impertinent, Mr Hewitt, but do you know how much the donation would have been worth?"

"I really don't think I should talk about this." Mr Hewitt's eyes darted between the women.

"Please, Mr Hewitt. This might be important and if you tell us now, it should stop the police coming to interview you later."

Mr Hewitt's eyes settled on Eliza. "Very well. It was for one thousand pounds."

"One thousand pounds?" Connie's voice rang out around the churchyard. "Good grief."

"But now you can't be sure whether you'll get the money because you don't know whether Mrs Milwood had already changed the will?"

"Exactly." Mr Hewitt shuffled his feet before moving to the door. "If you'll excuse me, I must be going." He pushed on the door but Eliza put an arm out to stop him.

"Before you go, can you tell me who was at home when you called at the Wilsons' house?"

"Well ... yes. Mrs Wilson, of course, and possibly her daughter, although I didn't see her. I was in the drawing room with Mrs Milwood."

"What about Mr Wilson?"

Mr Hewitt ran a hand across his face. "Possibly. He may have come home from work while we were talking, but I didn't see him."

"And so as far as you're aware, neither Mr nor Mrs Wilson knew anything about the donation."

Mr Hewitt shrugged. "I can't say for certain but she asked me not to say anything."

"Well, that certainly puts a new complexion on things."

Eliza raised her eyebrows at Connie and turned back to Mr Hewitt. "Was the vicar aware of this?"

"Only what I told him. He wasn't involved in the discussions."

Eliza's brow furrowed as her mind raced. "I don't doubt what you've said, Mr Hewitt, but would you mind if we have a quick word with the vicar? You said he was waiting for you, could we take a couple of minutes of his time?"

"I suppose so." With a deep sigh, Mr Hewitt pushed on the door and held it open for them.

"Is that you, Mr Hewitt?" The sound of the vicar's voice echoed off the walls. "What took you so long?"

He walked from his office into the church but stopped abruptly when he saw Eliza and Connie. "Oh, I do apologise, ladies. I'd no idea we had visitors."

"It's we who should apologise," Eliza said. "I'm afraid we're responsible for delaying Mr Hewitt."

"They wondered if they might have a word with you, Vicar," Mr Hewitt said.

The vicar nodded. "Of course, how can I help?"

"As we explained to Mr Hewitt, we're in the unusual position of helping the police with their inquiry into the death of Mrs Milwood."

The vicar, who had seemed distracted, suddenly lifted his head and gave them his full attention. "Oh, I say, I'm sure I know nothing of the wickedness that went on with poor Mrs Milwood."

"I'm sure you had nothing to do with it, but I wonder if you have any information that might help us identify the killer."

The vicar shuddered.

"For example, did you see any members of the household in the days leading up to the death?"

The vicar pressed his fingers together in front of his chest. "No, I'm afraid I didn't. Unless you include their attendance at church the previous Sunday, of course. The family were in the congregation as usual, with the exception of Samuel. I understand he's moved to Over Moreton."

"Yes, that's right, although we hear he may have come back to Moreton-on-Thames a few days before Mrs Milwood's death."

The vicar studied Eliza. "That I can neither confirm nor deny. I didn't see him, but naturally that doesn't mean he wasn't here."

"No, quite. Can I ask what you knew about the donation Mrs Milwood was planning to make to the church? Did you speak to her about it?"

The vicar shook his head. "No, all I know is what Mr Hewitt told me. We were delighted about it, obviously, and I had thanked her for her generosity."

Eliza's forehead creased. "Was she with Mr or Mrs Wilson at the time?"

The vicar closed his eyes. "It was a few weeks ago now. As I remember, Mrs Wilson was pushing the wheelchair, but she was distracted by her daughter and so she wasn't part of the conversation."

"And Mr Wilson?"

"Mr Wilson, Mr Wilson. Let me think. I recall he was further behind them talking to his youngest son."

"And so you don't think either of them heard you talking to Mrs Milwood?"

"No, I would say not, although I'm sure there wasn't much to hear. All I said was 'Thank you for your generosity.'"

Eliza's eyes narrowed. "And how did she respond?"

"Now you mention it, her reaction was rather strange. She put a hand on my arm and a finger to her lips and said, 'Please, say no more of it, Vicar.'"

"Thank you, that's most helpful."

"Do you think she'd hidden the donation from the family?" Mr Hewitt asked.

Eliza nodded. "My guess is that she had. We've spoken to Mr and Mrs Wilson numerous times this week and the subject of the church hasn't come up."

The vicar linked his fingers together in front of his chest. "Well, I suppose we won't always be foremost in people's minds. Will that be all?"

"Yes, we've taken up enough of your time for one afternoon ... assuming you didn't speak to anyone else in the family in the days leading up to the death?"

"No, I can safely say I didn't. The only person I spoke to from the house was Mrs Harris the cook, but that was on an entirely unrelated matter."

"Mrs Harris was here?"

Mr Hewitt nodded. "Yes, I can confirm she was here on the Wednesday afternoon Mrs Milwood died. I saw her leave the church and head back towards the house."

Eliza paused. "What time would that have been?"

Mr Hewitt raised his eyes to the ceiling. "Let me think. The clock had struck a quarter past two, so within five minutes of that."

"We were sitting on a bench near the police station

around that time. I didn't see her, did you?" Connie asked Eliza.

"No, I didn't. Mr Hewitt, do you remember which way she left?"

"She turned right out of the church and walked across the village green," Mr Hewitt said. "I couldn't tell whether she turned off to go back to the house or continued on the same path towards Over Moreton. The new pavilion blocks the view somewhat, you see."

"Yes, of course." Eliza nodded. "Well, thank you, gentlemen, you've been most helpful. We won't delay you any longer."

"Always a pleasure, ladies. I hope we see you in church tomorrow."

"We'll be here." Connie grinned at Eliza. "Won't we, Mrs Thomson?"

CHAPTER TWENTY

E liza and Connie left the church in silence, but as they reached the road, Eliza indicated to one of the benches overlooking the bowling green.

"Well, that was enlightening," she said as they took a seat.

"It most certainly was," Connie said. "Who'd have thought Mrs Milwood would offer to pay for the church repairs?"

"I'm more interested to find out if Judith or Mr Wilson were aware of it. It's hard to believe they weren't, and if another motive for murder was needed..."

Connie stared at Eliza, her mouth open. "You're not suggesting they killed Mrs Milwood to stop her from changing her will?"

"It's a common reason for killing someone. Judith said Mr Wilson had a copy of the will, which he'd put away for safekeeping. I think it's about time we asked to see it."

"Do you think that's why they were planning a move back to London despite Mrs Milwood's objections?"

Eliza screwed up her face. "It would make sense. I wonder

how serious they were about it though. Was it an empty threat or had they actually found somewhere to live?"

"I suppose we need to go back and ask them."

"We do, but not only to speak to them about that. Until now, we've been led to believe that Mrs Harris left the house shortly after midday to visit a friend in Over Moreton. From what we've just heard, she was still here at half past two."

"Yes, of course ... but why would she walk past the shop and across the village green? It would have been easier for her to walk on the road if she was going to either the house or Over Moreton."

"Why indeed. I wonder if she saw us sitting with Judith and didn't want us to see her." Eliza stood up. "I think it's about time we spoke to Mrs Harris, see what she has to say for herself."

"Now?"

Eliza turned to study the church clock. "We've got time to go to the police station first, seeing we're here, then we'll go to the Wilsons'. We should find out what the police have been doing."

Connie fell into step beside Eliza. "They said they were going to speak to the other son, Frank. He may be able to add something."

Eliza nodded. "I'm sure he can, although whether Sergeant Cooper has found out what that something is, remains to be seen."

"Good afternoon, ladies," Sergeant Cooper said as they walked into the station. "I didn't expect to see you today, with it being Saturday."

Eliza smiled. "Time and tide wait for no man, Sergeant. If there's a killer on the loose, we need to find him."

"Well, yes, indeed."

"We wondered if you had any more information for us. Did you speak to Frank?"

"I let Constable Jenkins do it." The sergeant appeared rather pleased with himself. "He's been keen to get in on the act, so to speak, and so I thought, what harm could it do letting him interview young Frank?"

Eliza struggled to keep a neutral expression. "And did he find out anything of interest?"

The sergeant's stature deflated. "No, nothing exciting. He confirmed that Frank had been at work on the day of the murder. He'd been at home for dinner the night before Mrs Milwood's death, but shortly afterwards he'd come up here for a few pints in the Golden Eagle. I happened to see him in there myself and so I can vouch for him."

"Remind me what he does for a living," Eliza said.

"He's a reporter with the local paper. Doing an apprenticeship, he is."

"That's right. Did you find out where he was working and confirm his alibi?"

The sergeant consulted his notebook. "He said he was working on a story about the theft of some meat in Over Moreton, but with the newspaper offices being closed today, we haven't been able to confirm it. Constable Jenkins will call on Monday to check with them."

Eliza nodded. "Yes, I don't suppose there's much he can do on a Saturday. If we see Frank in the meantime, we'll have a word with him. See if he gives us the same story. We'll call at the Wilsons' this afternoon; it occurred to us that we've not spoken to the cook yet. I presume you or Constable Jenkins haven't?"

"No, not yet. We didn't think she'd have much to say, being stuck in the kitchen every day."

It was all Eliza could do to stop her head from shaking. "Yes, we're probably wasting our time, but for completeness we should speak to everyone."

"Very good, Mrs Thomson. Let me know if you need any assistance."

"Yes, I will." Eliza turned to leave but stopped. "Actually, talking of help, have you heard when the inspector will be back?"

Sergeant Cooper pumped up his chest again. "I told him everything was under control so he said it won't be until Tuesday or Wednesday. Do you need to speak to him?"

"No, not at the moment, thank you, Sergeant."

Once they were outside the station, Eliza raised her head to the sky.

"What's the matter?" Connie asked.

"Nothing." Eliza chose her words carefully. "Sergeant Cooper's a lovely man, but why let the constable go out by himself."

"Don't you think he's doing a good job?"

Eliza noticed the concern in Connie's voice. "Yes, of course he is but Constable Jenkins is hardly going to make a detective. He needs assistance. Come on, let's go and see what Mrs Harris has to say."

By the time they arrived at the Wilsons' house, Mrs Harris was preparing dinner. Judith showed them into the kitchen but at Eliza's request left them alone to talk to the cook.

"My, this looks a busy kitchen," Eliza said.

"It is." Mrs Harris didn't look up. "I can't stand around talking, just because it's Saturday."

Eliza stood by the table and watched as Mrs Harris beat several eggs into a butter and sugar mixture. "Is that going to be a Victoria sandwich cake?"

"If I get a minute to make it, it is. Now, are you going to tell me why you're here so I can get on?"

"Yes, indeed. We'd like to ask you a few questions about the death of Mrs Milwood."

"Don't ask me." Mrs Harris straightened the white cotton cap covering her head before she picked up a bowl of flour and began folding it into the mixture.

"I'm sure we won't take much of your time," Connie said. "We're helping the police with their inquiries and we need to speak to everyone in the household. You may know something you don't realise is important."

Mrs Harris snorted. "I doubt it, what is it you want to know?"

"On the morning of Mrs Milwood's death, Mrs Wilson says you were in the kitchen as usual," Eliza said.

"I was. In here at half past six on the dot ready to make Mr Wilson his breakfast."

"Did Mr Wilson come in here any time that morning or look particularly tired when you saw him?"

"Of course he didn't come in here. Does your husband ever venture into the kitchen?"

"No, of course not, but we needed to check. What about his appearance? Did he look as if he'd had a good night's sleep?"

Mrs Harris shrugged. "Didn't take much notice to tell you the truth. I would say he looked the same as usual."

"What about Mrs Wilson?" Connie asked. "Was Mr Wilson still at home when she arrived for breakfast?"

Mrs Harris blew out through her lips. "After the argument they'd had over breakfast the day before, I'd say she deliberately waited until he'd gone out. He was long gone before she came downstairs."

"They'd argued?" Connie turned to Eliza.

"They're always arguing, although they try to hide it from everyone. She wants to go back to London and he wants to stay here so as not to threaten his inheritance."

"And is that what they argued about the day before the murder?"

"Pretty much, although Mrs Wilson was more forceful than usual. I heard her say that she didn't care about the money and that if she had to get a job when they moved, then she would."

Connie's eyes were wide. "How did Mr Wilson respond to that?"

"He told her she'd be going on her own and stormed off to work. He didn't even finish his breakfast."

"Was Mrs Wilson upset when you served her breakfast?" Eliza said.

Mrs Harris shrugged. "I gave her a minute to collect herself, but by the time I went into the dining room, she'd gone. Back to her room, I presumed."

"How terrible," Connie said.

"And how was she with Mr Wilson when he arrived home that evening?" Eliza said. "Did they argue again?"

Mrs Harris hesitated. "No, they didn't, it was quite strange. She was waiting for him when he came home and ushered him straight into the drawing room. I couldn't hear what they said because neither was shouting but when they sat down for dinner half an hour later, they were both tense."

"Did Mrs Milwood join them?"

The cook shook her head. "She didn't, but I didn't expect her to after the accusations Mrs Wilson had hurled at her less than an hour earlier. A right to-do it was."

"Go on," Eliza said. "What did Mrs Wilson say?"

Mrs Harris paused. "I'm sure I shouldn't tell tales like this."

Eliza put a hand on Mrs Harris' shoulder. "Please go on. The police will need to know what happened and so you can either tell us now or they'll want to question you."

Mrs Harris rolled her shoulders. "If you put it like that, I suppose you're the lesser of the two evils. To start with Mrs Wilson said she'd had enough of doing the duties of a maid and that it was about time they had someone to replace Ruby."

"That's not unreasonable," Connie said.

"But they'd been without a maid for nearly a month," Eliza said. "Why do you think Mrs Wilson chose that day to bring it up with Mrs Milwood?"

Mrs Harris shrugged. "How would I know?"

"But you have an idea?"

"I don't think Ruby's replacement was the main reason for the argument. Shortly beforehand, Mr Hewitt from church had called, and by the sound of it, Mrs Milwood had promised a large sum of money to the church. Mrs Wilson must have overheard because she said that if the old lady was giving their inheritance away, there was no reason for them to stay."

So Judith knew about it.

"That might explain what she wanted to talk to Mr Wilson about when he came in that evening," Connie said.

"It could have been." Cook nodded and softened her

voice. "It's a terrible thing to say, but it wouldn't surprise me if either of them murdered Mrs Milwood, not that I'd blame them if they did. She made their lives miserable. Mr Wilson told her as much later that evening."

"Mr Wilson argued with his mother as well?" Eliza stared at Mrs Harris. "Did anyone ever have a civil conversation? What did he say?"

"Not lately they didn't, but when Mr Wilson spoke to his mother, I was making dinner and so only heard the end of it. It sounded like they were arguing about the donation and Mr Wilson said they were leaving."

"So Mrs Wilson must have told him. What time was this?"

The cook paused again to think. "Mr Wilson was home from work and I hadn't heard the church bells for a while and so it must have been close to half past five."

Eliza nodded. "Well, thank you, Mrs Harris, you've been most helpful. Can I ask one final question? How was your relationship with Mrs Milwood? Did you get along with her?"

Cook pulled herself up to her full height. "I think I was the only one who did. She always treated me well and did me no harm. I'm sorry she's gone, especially if it means the Wilsons will move back to London. I'll be out of a job."

"Yes, of course, I hadn't thought of that," Connie said. "Let's hope they stay now they can have a more peaceful life here."

CHAPTER TWENTY-ONE

With the Sunday morning service over, Eliza, Connie and Archie passed through the church door to be greeted by the vicar.

"Lovely service, Vicar," Connie said as she accepted the vicar's handshake.

"Thank you, Mrs Appleton, and with Dr and Mrs Thomson too. It's delightful to see you here again. Tell me, how are your investigations coming along? Have you found out yet who committed the terrible crime?"

A cloud crossed Eliza's face as the vicar shook her hand. "Not yet, but we're getting a clearer picture of what might have happened. I'm sure the whole village will find out soon enough once an arrest is made."

"Well, I shall keep you ladies and the police officers in my prayers. Villagers need to know they can sleep safely in their beds at night."

"They do indeed. Good day, Vicar."

As they passed through the church gate, Eliza scowled at Connie. "Did you seriously enjoy that service?"

Connie smirked. "Of course not, but I was taught to always be polite."

"And I was taught that if you haven't got anything nice to say, you should keep quiet. You shouldn't encourage him."

"It wasn't that bad," Archie said as Eliza linked her arm in his.

"Wasn't that bad ... were you in the same service as me?"

Archie chuckled. "Quite possibly not, I was thinking about the roast chicken Cook has in the oven."

Connie took a deep breath of the warm air. "I don't care what you say about the service. It's nice to sit quietly and have a day off from questioning everyone."

"Don't you enjoy it?" Archie asked.

"Oh, yes, of course I do, but it's exhausting. I'm sure Eliza doesn't worry about it, but I'm not used to it."

"It's a good job you're joining us for Sunday dinner then," Eliza said. "You can have the whole day off."

With the food served and Iris and Cook back in the kitchen, Archie raised the subject of the investigation.

"It feels like I haven't spoken to you for days. Do you have a suspect yet?"

Eliza put down her knife and fork. "The problem is, there are a lot of suspects but at the moment Judith or Mr Wilson seem to have the most reason for wanting Mrs Milwood out of the way. They also clearly had the opportunity to poison her."

"Although we can't rule out Sam," Connie said.

"Has he still not turned up?"

Eliza took a mouthful of roast potato and shook her head. "No, and I must say the longer he stays away, the worse it looks for him. Why else would he disappear on the day his grandmother was murdered?"

"Does he have a motive?"

Eliza sighed and once again put down her cutlery. "He does. We've found out he was secretly walking out with the housemaid, Ruby, and when Mrs Milwood found out she sacked Ruby and found her a job miles away in Over Moreton and threatened to disinherit Sam."

Archie glanced up from his plate. "Is that why Sam left home?"

"It is, but given he was still seeing Ruby, is that reason to murder someone?"

"If Mrs Milwood had as much money as is rumoured, being disinherited is a powerful motivator."

"You're right. It's Ruby I feel sorry for; she's worried sick about him."

Archie took a sip from his cup of tea. "I forgot to tell you, I got the results back from the laboratory yesterday about that herbal medicine you found at the Wilsons'."

Eliza's voice squeaked as she spoke. "You forgot!"

"I've hardly seen you."

"What did it say? Did it contain digitalis?"

"It did, but only in low doses."

With her appetite gone, Eliza pushed her plate into the centre of the table. "Too low to kill her?"

"Almost certainly," Archie said, "especially as the bottle was nearly full. Even if she'd had heart problems, I doubt the amount missing would have killed her. It wouldn't account for the levels found in her blood."

"So that takes us back to square one." Eliza sat back in her chair. "Where on earth did the digitalis come from that killed her?"

All three remained silent as Iris came back into the room to tidy away the dishes. Moments later, she returned with a large dish of apple crumble.

"How lovely," Connie said as Eliza served her a portion. "I rarely make puddings for myself. It doesn't seem worth it."

"Well, there's plenty here and so you can take some home with you. I'll get Cook to make you a bit of custard to go with it."

Connie smiled. "You're good to me. I can hardly believe it's only two weeks tomorrow since you moved back. So much has happened, it's as if you were never away."

"It is rather. It's such fun though, being able to help the police."

"It is as long as we don't do it every week. I don't want any more dead bodies turning up." Connie shuddered. "This is the first murder we've ever had around here."

"That doesn't surprise me, the way the police..." Eliza turned to Archie. "Who's the doctor in Over Moreton? There must be one, you don't work over there."

"A chap named Wark. I've not met him yet."

"We need to check whether he's had any digitalis taken from his dispensary. If Sam had anything to do with the murder, or if Ruby was an accomplice, they may have been more likely to take it from him, not you. Besides, if it was premeditated, we only arrived two days beforehand. Dr Wark was already here."

"Sam was seen helping the removals men here though, don't forget," Connie said. "He could have taken your bottle if he'd needed it."

"He could, but if he'd already made his plans ... I wonder..."

Archie put a hand on his wife's. "Now look what you've done, Mrs Appleton. You've set her thinking. I won't be able to do anything with her for the rest of the afternoon."

Connie's cheeks flushed as Archie smiled at her, but Eliza said nothing. After a moment's silence, she turned to her husband.

"Will you go and see this Dr Wark tomorrow and ask if he's missing any digitalis? It has to have come from somewhere."

Archie raised his eyes to the ceiling. "If it gets me out of the house, how can I refuse!"

CHAPTER TWENTY-TWO

Monday morning was drawing to a close when Eliza picked up the final prescription. Not for the first time she puzzled over her husband's handwriting, *paste of …* *magnesium sulphate?* Yes, that must be it. It was for Mrs Harris, she'd been in with a rash on her hands. Too much washing-up now she was on her own. As she reached for the jar, the door to the dispensary opened and Sergeant Cooper and Constable Jenkins walked in.

"Ah, Mrs Thomson. Your maid said we'd find you here."

"Good morning to you both. To what do I owe the pleasure?"

The sergeant coughed to clear his throat. "We're here to tell you that young Samuel Wilson turned up in the village this morning and that we've arrested him for the murder of Mrs Milwood."

The blood drained from Eliza's face as she looked between the officers. "You've arrested him? On what grounds?"

"On what grounds?" Constable Jenkins gave the sergeant

an incredulous look. "Because his grandmother was murdered on the day he disappeared. If that isn't evidence enough, then I don't know what is."

"Do you have a confession?"

Sergeant Cooper's face fell. "No, not yet, but don't you worry, we'll get one."

"You can't say that. He may be perfectly innocent. Did you ask him where he's been? And more importantly, why he came back?"

"He went to London," Constable Jenkins said.

"And...?"

"He went to London to get away from here."

Eliza's eyes widened. "You can't arrest someone for going to London. Let me get my coat ... and Mrs Appleton. We need to speak to him."

Eliza didn't wait for a response before she hurried from the room to collect her coat. Two minutes later she was at Connie's door.

"Get your coat, we need to go to the police station."

When Connie hesitated Eliza glanced back to the surgery where the officers were waiting. "Don't ask questions, just do it. The police have arrested Sam and we need to go and see him."

"But you said you didn't think he did it."

"I don't, that's why we have to be quick. I don't want them questioning him without us being there."

The sergeant and Constable Jenkins stopped their conversation when they returned.

"Don't you think we should have arrested him?" Sergeant Cooper asked.

"No, I don't." Eliza's chest was burning from the pace she

had been walking at. "I think it would have been appropriate to question him, but not lock him up."

The sergeant glared at his constable. "What did I tell you? Wait for Mrs Thomson and Mrs Appleton, I said, but you wouldn't listen."

"Who's in charge here, Sergeant?" Eliza's tone was curt.

"It's as clear as day that he's the culprit," Jenkins said. "Why am I the only one who can see it?"

"Is he in the cell at the back?" Eliza asked as they entered the police station.

"He is."

Eliza's pace slowed and before he saw her, Eliza watched Sam as he sat on the side of the stone bed, his fingers pushed into dark curls as he held his head in his hands. Eliza motioned for Connie to introduce her.

Connie nodded. "Good morning, Sam. Do you mind if we talk to you for a few minutes? We'd like to help you."

Sam's dark eyes were filled with fear.

"This is Mrs Thomson," Connie continued. "She's the doctor's wife and a friend of your mother's. We're helping the police with their inquiries."

"Then you need to get me out of here. I've done nothing wrong." Sam launched himself at the bars. "They told me Grandmother's dead and they think I killed her, but I don't know what they're talking about." He glared at Constable Jenkins, who stood on guard outside the door to the cell.

Eliza turned to the sergeant. "Would you mind giving us a few minutes alone with Sam? We'll call if we need you."

The sergeant's brow creased. "You mean you want me to let you into the cell and leave you unaccompanied?"

Eliza studied the young man with tousled hair and sallow skin.

"Yes, please. He's nothing but a frightened young man, he won't do us any harm, will you, Sam?"

Sam shook his head as Sergeant Cooper looked from him to Eliza and back again before reluctantly reaching for his keys. "I'm not happy about this. I'll position myself by the door should you need any help."

"Thank you, but I'm sure that won't be necessary."

"Necessary or not, I'm not leaving two ladies in here alone with him. He's already committed one murder."

"We don't know that."

Sergeant Cooper withered under Eliza's glare. "No, of course ... not yet." He held the door to the cell open for them. "But it's only a matter of time."

With the sergeant outside the room, Sam grabbed Connie's hands. "Mrs Appleton, please tell me what's happening. Is it true about my grandmother?"

Connie sighed. "Yes, I'm afraid it is. Your mother found her murdered in her bed a week last Wednesday."

"Murdered? How?"

"Poisoned." Eliza's face was stern.

"Poisoned? I wouldn't know how to poison anyone. Why do they think it was me?"

"Because on the day they found her, you left work at around midday and nobody's seen you since. Constable Jenkins thinks that alone is enough to convict you, but I happen to think differently. We'd like to help, but to do that, you must be perfectly honest with us."

Sam's mouth opened and closed several times before he

spoke. "But I didn't do anything. I'd planned a trip to London ... I didn't know it would look suspicious."

"Can you tell us what time you left and how you travelled?" Eliza said.

"I took the train. The afternoon train."

"It leaves Over Moreton at five past three," Connie said in response to Eliza's expression. "Before Mrs Milwood's body was found."

Eliza was silent as Sam jumped from his seat. "That doesn't mean I killed her."

"Sam, please, come and sit down." Eliza glanced at the sergeant as he stood at ease in front of the outer door. "I need to ask you some questions and we don't want to bring the sergeant in here." Her voice was low as she spoke and after a second's hesitation Sam returned to his seat.

"We've been to see Ruby," Eliza whispered.

Sam closed his eyes and took a deep breath. "Does she think I did it?"

"No. No, she doesn't."

Sam's sigh of relief was audible. "I did it for her."

"You murdered your grandmother for Ruby?" Connie's eyes were wide.

"No!" Sam ran a hand through his hair. "I went to London for her."

"But you didn't tell her what you were doing? She thought she'd upset you and that you didn't want to see her again."

"Of course I want to see her again."

"Well, why did you leave without telling her?" Connie asked.

Sam's high-pitched voice softened. "I want her to be my wife."

Eliza and Connie stared at each other.

"You'd asked her to marry you?" Connie said.

"She didn't mention anything about it to us," Eliza added.

"No, I hadn't asked her ... I wanted to surprise her." He reached into the inside pocket of his jacket and pulled out a piece of paper. "This is why I went to London."

Eliza took the paper and unfolded it. "A marriage licence."

"I couldn't get it until yesterday. I had to live in London for at least a week before I was eligible. Otherwise I'd have got it on the first day and come straight back."

Eliza passed the document to Connie. "Where did you get the money from for this, not to mention the payment for the train fare?"

"I have a job..."

"And I reckon that once you'd paid a month's rent to hold your room open, there wouldn't be much money to spare."

Sam's mouth fell open.

Eliza patted his hand. "A lot of people have been looking for you. Of course we know about the rent, but we also know you planned on visiting your grandmother on the afternoon she died."

"How did you know that? The only person who knew..."

"Was Ruby," Eliza said. "And yes, she's been worried sick about you ever since she heard about the death and your disappearance."

Sam put his head in his hands and Eliza lowered her voice further.

"We've also learned that a large sum of money was taken from your grandmother's house around the time of her death. Enough to pay your rent and the expenses for the trip, I would say. Did you go and ask her for some money, or did you just take it?"

Sam remained silent.

"Your parents are worried that you took the money before poisoning your grandmother," Connie said.

Sam's voice was barely audible. "No. I wouldn't. Please, you must believe me." His dark eyes were like pools of chocolate as he pleaded with them.

"Did you think life with Ruby would be easier with your grandmother out of the way?"

"No." Sam wiped a finger across his eyes. "I realise all this doesn't look very good, but I swear I didn't kill her."

Eliza and Connie sat in silence as he struggled with his next words.

"I admit I did call on her that afternoon. I wanted to borrow some money, but when I got there, she was in bed. She told me she wasn't feeling well and asked if I could fetch a bottle of herbal medicine for her."

"You gave her some herbal medicine?" Eliza raised an eyebrow at him. "How much?"

Sam shrugged. "Not much, only a spoonful in some water."

"And that was all?"

"Yes, why?"

"You may recall my husband and I moved into the surgery two days before your grandmother was murdered. On the Monday to be precise. I understand you were outside the surgery with your sister and that you helped the removals men carry some boxes inside. What were you doing and why weren't you at work?"

Sam looked from Eliza to Connie. "I wasn't doing anything."

"Well, can you tell me why you took two bottles of medicine from the boxes being carried into the surgery? What did you intend doing with them?"

Connie's mouth fell open while Sam's face flushed scarlet.

"I ... I didn't do anything with them ... I just found them and picked them up ... I didn't even know what they were ... honestly."

"So they were just lying on the floor? Why didn't you take them into the surgery? That would have been the sensible thing to do."

"I was going to, but ... but at that minute, Flora called and I forgot."

"Ah, yes, Flora. Her presence was going to be my next question. What did she want?"

"She didn't want anything. I hadn't seen her for a few weeks and she was surprised to see me."

"Yes, you still haven't explained why you weren't at work."

Sam sat in silence causing Eliza to study the notebook on her lap.

"All right, I suspect there are still things you haven't told me, which is unfortunate because you're making it difficult for us to help you. Let me recap on what we know. Two days before your grandmother's death, you were inexplicably in Moreton-on-Thames during working hours. You're lying about the bottles of medicine being on the ground, because I unpacked that box, and it was not damaged in any way. There's no chance those bottles fell to the ground." Eliza once again checked to see Sergeant Cooper standing at ease. "If I were the police, I'd assume you deliberately took those bottles with the intention of murdering your grandmother."

"No!"

Eliza held up her hand to silence him. "The only thing in your favour so far is that you didn't take the two bottles next to them in the box. Alongside the chloroform and codeine you took was a bottle of digitalis pills and another containing a tincture of digitalis, medicines known for their toxic effects and both containing the drug that killed your grandmother."

Sam gulped and looked from one to the other. "I didn't do anything with the bottles and didn't touch any others. When I remembered I had them, I hid them in the garden and rushed off to catch the train."

"So I presume this was after you saw your grandmother ... and had taken her money? It would be easy for the police to suggest that you visited your grandmother to ask for some money, but she refused and you lost your temper. You've admitted you already had the chloroform in your pocket. How do we know you didn't soak a cloth in the liquid and hold it over her mouth before you stole her money?"

"Because I wouldn't ... I couldn't. How could I do that?"

"Quite easily if she was sleeping ... and she would have breathed it off by the time she passed away."

"But she wasn't sleeping ... I told you."

"Well, perhaps you gave her some codeine tablets knowing she had only recently taken her own. She had traceable levels of codeine in her system, you see."

"No!" Sam jumped to his feet. "How would I do that? I couldn't force her to take any tablets if she wasn't ready for them. She always knew when every tablet was to be taken."

"Is everything all right in here, ladies?" Sergeant Cooper glared at Sam as he stood over Eliza and Connie.

"Yes, thank you, Sergeant. You've no need to worry, we're just having a discussion." Eliza waited for the sergeant to go back to the outer room before turning back to Sam. "You have to see how this looks. I'm not sure I can convince the police to release you at the moment, but if you think of anything else, you must tell me."

Sam wiped a hand across his forehead.

"We want to help you, but we can't if you won't tell us the truth," Connie said. "Please, trust us."

Sam took a deep breath and sat back down. "All right, let me tell you what happened. I admit I was angry with her and the thought of killing her had crossed my mind. But that was all. I didn't do it. I was angry with her. It was so much harder to be with Ruby when she was at the manor house, even though I'd moved to Over Moreton, and my money wasn't lasting as long as I'd hoped either.

"When I saw the medicines going into the surgery, I couldn't resist the temptation to take some, even though I didn't know what they were."

"But Flora would have done," Eliza interrupted. "Is that what you were talking about?"

Sam stared at her.

"We've been to the room in the attic she uses as a study," Eliza said. "There are a lot of medical books up there."

Sam shook his head. "No, leave Flora out of this. It had nothing to do with her. It was my idea. When Father left work on the Wednesday, I followed him. I wanted to talk to him about Ruby, but instead of going for a walk as he often does, he headed towards the train station. That was when I decided to talk to Grandmother. I also needed some money and so I thought I'd ask her instead of Father. I meant it when I said she was ill. I helped her take some medicine and arranged her pillows for her. She looked as if she was going to sleep and so I slipped into Mr Milwood's old study to see if I could still get into the safe. When it opened, I took a handful of notes and left as quickly as I could."

Eliza studied Sam, but said nothing.

"Please, you have to believe me. I might not be not sorry she's dead, but I didn't kill her. I just couldn't do it. Besides, why would I come back if I was guilty? It would have made more sense to take Ruby with me and never come back."

"It would," Eliza said, never taking her eyes off Sam. "Why would you come back, if you'd killed your grandmother?"

CHAPTER TWENTY-THREE

E liza pushed herself from her seat and picked up her handbag.

"You've not made things easy for us," she said to Sam, "but I do believe you. We'll have to check your movements with everyone who may have seen you though."

Sam nodded and lowered his head but immediately jerked it up when the sergeant came into the room.

"Another visitor for the prisoner." Sergeant Cooper ushered the young man into the room before resuming his guard on the door.

A smile flashed across Sam's face when his brother walked into the room.

"Frank! Have you come to get me out of here?"

Frank gazed at the faces staring at him. "I've come to see how you are and find out why you've been locked up."

Eliza put her bag back onto the table and nudged Connie, who took a step forward.

"Good afternoon, Frank. I'm sure you remember me, but

can I introduce Mrs Thomson, Dr Thomson's wife? We're helping the police with their inquiries into your grandmother's death."

Eliza gave him a subdued smile. "It seems your brother's in a spot of bother. The police believe he was responsible for your grandmother's death, which is why they've arrested him. Do you have any information that may help?"

Frank's eyes searched the pleading face of his brother. "They accused you of murdering the old dame? How on earth did that happen? You've not even been here."

"That's not strictly true," Eliza said. "Mrs Milwood was poisoned sometime between one and six o'clock in the early hours of Wednesday morning. She died later that day. There would have been plenty of time for your brother to have administered the poison and then taken a train to London to get out of the way. Unfortunately for him, the fact that he disappeared on the day of her death looks very suspicious."

Frank studied his brother but didn't speak.

"You don't seem surprised, Frank," Connie said.

Frank gave her a blank stare. "Don't seem surprised? I'm in a state of shock."

"Why don't you tell us a little about yourself then?" Eliza said. "You're the only member of the family we haven't spoken to yet."

"Me? What do you want to know?"

"You're training to be a journalist, I believe. Are you close to being allowed to work unsupervised?"

Frank relaxed. "I should be by the end of the year."

"And then what?" Eliza asked.

Frank shrugged. "I'd hoped to go back to London. I've

always fancied working on Fleet Street, on one of the national newspapers."

"Was your grandmother happy about that?"

"She was fine ... and my parents were. Why?"

It was Eliza's turn to shrug. "It's probably of no consequence but you seem to be the only member of the family whose life your grandmother didn't interfere with. Did you know she disapproved of Sam's friendship with your maid Ruby?"

"You and Ruby?" Frank smirked at his brother. "You dark horse. Is that why Ruby moved to the manor house?"

Sam nodded.

"And I presume you knew how opposed your grandmother was to Flora taking a place at university," Eliza continued.

Frank chuckled. "You didn't have to be a journalist to work that out. I reckon everyone who visited the house must have known."

"So what can you tell us about your parents?"

"My parents? What about them?"

"How did they respond to being told they couldn't leave Moreton and go back to London?"

"I'm not sure they wanted to go..."

"Really?" Eliza raised an eyebrow. "You're training to be a journalist but hadn't realised how desperately unhappy your mother was, or that your father had applied for his old job back in London?"

"N-no. I work long hours and spend most evenings at the Golden Eagle. I didn't see much of them."

Eliza turned on her heel to pace the floor. "That's a

shame. Your brother could do with your help right now. Never mind, tell me about your grandmother. I've heard she was a wealthy woman, but I haven't heard how she came by her money."

Frank shrugged. "There's not much to tell. Several years after our grandfather died, she married Mr Milwood. He was a self-made man and when he died, he left her his money and business."

Eliza glanced at Connie. "Mrs Milwood owned a business?"

Connie's cheeks turned pink. "She did, and it didn't occur to me to mention it. Is it important?"

"It may or may not be, but we won't know unless we examine all the evidence." Eliza turned back to Frank. "What was the name of your grandmother's business?"

"Moreton Industries."

"I've heard that name before." Eliza reached for her notebook and flicked through it.

"It's where Father used to work," Sam said. "Before we came back here."

Eliza scratched her head. "Your father worked for your grandmother's company? As an employee or on the board of directors?"

"He was finance director," Sam said.

Connie's brow creased. "Does that mean he holds shares in the company?"

"And if he did, why was he unable to get his old job back?" Eliza studied the three sets of eyes watching her. "Unless..."

"He didn't know." Frank gasped.

"Didn't know what?" Eliza cocked her head to one side.

Frank held up his hands. "All right, I admit, I knew he'd asked for his old job back. I was researching a story on bank fraud a couple of weeks ago and a found a snippet of information saying that Grandmother had blocked the appointment of a new finance director. That's when I learned that Father had written to the chairman. He runs the business for Grandmother but would write her a weekly report. I found one of the reports and realised it was Father she had turned down."

"But you didn't tell him?"

Frank's eyes were wide. "How could I? There was already enough tension in the house, I couldn't risk adding to it."

"But that doesn't confirm he hadn't found out some other way."

"No, you're wrong, I'd swear that had he known, we'd all have heard about it."

"Because he would have said something?"

"Of course he would, wouldn't you if you found out something like that?"

As Eliza scribbled in her notepad, Connie turned to Frank. "On the day of Mrs Milwood's death, your father said he travelled to London to find out why they turned him down for the job. They could have told him then."

Eliza stopped her writing. "They may have done, but Mrs Milwood was poisoned before he left for London, not once he got back. If he only found out in London, it wouldn't be a motive for murder. It does pose two questions though. First, assuming he now knows, when did he find out? And second, why on earth didn't he mention it?" Eliza put her hands to her head. "I really don't know what to make of all this. We're trying to defend people who refuse to give us all the facts."

She paused to study the two young men in front of her. "This doesn't let Sam off the hook, but it confuses the evidence somewhat. I'm going to visit your parents now, and Flora. I need the truth from everyone, and if either of you have anything else to say, I'd be obliged if you'd tell me."

CHAPTER TWENTY-FOUR

A s they left the police station, Eliza nodded towards the benches opposite.

"Do you mind if we sit and catch our breath? I'm exhausted after that."

"Not at all," Connie said. "I hope Sergeant Cooper's lenient with poor Sam."

"I think he will be. He didn't say anything, but I imagine he was listening in to most of the conversation. It's the constable we need to watch."

"Do you really think Sam's innocent?" Connie asked as they sat down.

Eliza's brow furrowed. "I'm not certain, but I'd say so. He did look genuinely surprised when we told him about his grandmother, and as he said, if he'd given her the poison, why come back?"

"Maybe he was missing home, or Ruby more like it."

"Possibly."

Connie stayed silent before turning to her friend. "How did you know it was Sam who'd taken the medicine bottles?"

Eliza grinned. "I didn't, but it made sense. The removals men had been in and out of the surgery all afternoon and for whatever reason he'd been helping them. Despite what everyone wanted me to think, the box hadn't been damaged and so someone must have deliberately taken them. Flora gave it away. She was very vague about what Sam was doing at the surgery, and I realised she could have helped him choose which bottles to take. I decided to test my theory, and it turned out to be right."

"So, do you think Flora's involved?"

Eliza let out a deep sigh. "That's a big question. I certainly think she knew what Sam was up to, but was she an accomplice? Possibly. It's a question of whether she could have given the poison when Sam lost his nerve."

"No, surely not!" Connie gasped. "She's a young girl."

"That's as may be, but she's determined to go to university and poisons are most commonly used by women who want to be rid of someone. The fact she wants to study medicine and has a room full of scientific textbooks doesn't help her innocence. We need to speak to her."

Connie shuddered. "What a terrible state of affairs. I never imagined it would be so complicated."

"Neither did I." Eliza patted Connie's hand. "Often the police struggle to find one person with a motive and opportunity to commit murder, but in this case, it feels as if everyone we talk to could have done it."

"At least the inspector should be back tomorrow. Will you tell him what we've found out so far and leave it to him?"

Eliza shot Connie a look of alarm, which caused her friend to laugh. "I most certainly will not."

"Well, we've been at this for nearly two weeks and we're no closer to finding the culprit."

"I will not be defeated. Come along." Eliza stood up and stepped onto the footpath. "Nobody in the Wilson household is telling us the whole truth and so before we do anything else, we'll pay them another visit."

"Now? Haven't we done enough for one day?"

"Under normal circumstances, I would say yes, but we can't let this hang. It only needs Frank to go home and tell Judith and Mr Wilson what's going on and they could make up another story."

"You don't think Mr Wilson would kill his own mother, do you?" Connie asked.

Eliza sighed. "I didn't, but now I'm not so sure. He certainly had a motive. We need to find out what he knew about Mrs Milwood stopping his move back to London."

"Or what Judith knew," Connie said. "She was so desperate to leave here, you don't think..."

"That she's our poisoner?" Eliza's smile disappeared. "I hope not, but all of a sudden, it can't be ruled out. She would easily have had access to Mrs Milwood's room in the middle of the night."

"So what do we do?"

Eliza started walking. "We go and tell them that if they're serious about wanting our help, they have to start telling us the truth. This has gone on for long enough. Come on, let's get it over with."

· · ·

Eliza stood back as Connie rattled the door-knocker of the Wilsons' front door. Judith opened it a crack and peered through.

"Oh, it's you."

"We're sorry to call so late. May we come in?" Connie said. "We need to talk."

Judith hesitated before pulling the door open. "Haven't we spoken enough?"

Eliza sighed as she stepped into the hallway. "I'm sure we have, but I'm afraid to say we're here as the bearers of bad news. Sam's been arrested and is in custody at the police station."

"Sam!"

"I'm afraid so. He came back to Moreton this morning and as soon as the police saw him they placed him under arrest."

"But why? Did you tell them about the money?"

"No, we hadn't mentioned that. It's because he disappeared on the day of Mrs Milwood's death."

"But that's no reason to arrest him; my poor boy." Judith reached for her coat. "I must go to him."

Eliza put a hand out and let it rest on top of the coat stand. "I'd rather you didn't, not yet, we need to talk first. And to Flora and Mr Wilson."

"I'm sure that can wait..."

"No, it can't. Is Mr Wilson home?"

Judith hesitated. "It's too early yet."

"Well, while we're waiting, can you fetch Flora? I think she knows a lot more about this case than she's admitting, and we're at a stage where everyone needs to start telling the truth."

Judith glanced from Eliza to Connie. "Flora does?"

Eliza nodded.

"Very well." Without argument, Judith turned to make her way upstairs.

"Do you think they'll tell us the truth?" Connie asked once she was out of sight.

"I do hope so, because I don't want to get cross with them. I thought it would be fun working out who the murderer was; I never expected so many lies or half-truths."

"I hope Judith's not the murderer ... not that I want Mr Wilson to be either, but..."

"What's this?" Eliza picked up a notepad that was resting on the console table and flicked through it.

"You can't read other people's things."

"This is a murder investigation, we can't worry about niceties." Eliza's pace slowed as she turned the pages until she paused towards the end of the book. "It's Frank's reporting notepad. How helpful that he dates everything so carefully."

Eliza was still reading when Connie nudged her ribs. She looked up and fixed Judith with a stare. "Ah, here you are."

"What are you doing with that?"

"All in good time. Shall we go into the drawing room?" Eliza didn't wait for Judith to respond and led the way with Connie in her wake. Flora stayed where she was until Eliza turned to shut the door.

"You as well, young lady. I've a feeling you know more than you've told us."

Eliza waited for Flora to take a seat and sat beside her. "I've just told your mother Sam's currently in police custody, charged with murdering your grandmother."

A gasp escaped from Flora's throat. "No."

Eliza nodded. "If it's any consolation, I don't think he did it, but the case against him is strong. Unless we find the real culprit, he could be in a lot of trouble. I know we've spoken to you before but I suspect you haven't been telling us the whole truth. This time, if we're to help Sam, I need you to tell me everything, honestly. Is that clear?"

Flora nodded. "He didn't do anything."

Eliza patted the girl's hand. "I understand you're trying to protect him, but by continually misleading us, you're actually making things worse. We know the two of you were up to something on the Monday afternoon before your grandmother died. Do you want to tell us what happened?"

"Sam found..."

"No, I'm sorry, I mustn't be making myself clear. Let me help." Eliza took a deep breath. "You and Sam were outside the surgery on the day the doctor and I moved into the village. We have witnesses who saw Sam helping the removals men carry boxes into the surgery, but when I came to unpack, two of the bottles were missing. Now, I know those bottles were packed alphabetically and the boxes hadn't been damaged, which means they couldn't have accidentally fallen out onto the garden path."

Flora's hands fidgeted in her lap.

"Sam's admitted to us that he took them with the intention of using them on your grandmother. The thing is, he had no idea what to do with them. That's where you come in. You constantly have your head in medical textbooks and would know exactly what the drugs were for. Was that the plan? To tell Sam about the medicines and get him to smother your grandmother with a chloroform-soaked handkerchief, or force a lethal dose of codeine tablets into her?"

Judith stared at her daughter. "You didn't?"

"No, we didn't. Neither of us." Flora jumped from her seat. "I'll admit we originally planned to use them, but we couldn't do it."

"Good, we're making progress," Eliza said. "Now, Sam has also admitted that he came here to see your grandmother on the Wednesday afternoon, when you were the only other person in the house. Did you see him?"

Flora nodded. "That was when we realised we couldn't go through with it and he said he'd put the bottles back in the surgery garden. He made me promise not to tell anyone."

"What else did he tell you? Please, be honest."

Flora glanced at her mother and took a deep breath. "He told me he was going to London and needed some money."

"And so not only did you know where he'd gone, you knew he'd taken money from the safe?"

Flora slumped back into the chair nearest her. "I didn't want to get him into trouble."

Eliza gave a gentle shake of her head. "Sadly, by not speaking up, you've quite possibly got him into more trouble than if you'd told the truth. Did he tell you about his friendship with Ruby and why he'd gone to London?"

Judith glared at her daughter. "What about Ruby? What's going on?"

"I'm sorry to say, Judith, that you know very little about what goes on under your own roof," Eliza said. "Several months ago, your son fell in love with the domestic help. Unfortunately for them, Mrs Milwood found out and sent Ruby to work at the manor house in Over Moreton. That's why Sam left soon afterwards."

"Sam and Ruby?" Judith turned to Flora. "And you knew?"

Flora moved to the seat on the settee beside her mother. "I'm sorry, don't be angry with me. He didn't tell me straight away, but then he needed to come here for some money. He told me he wanted to go to London ... and get a marriage licence."

"A marriage licence? He can't marry a servant!"

"It appears that was Mrs Milwood's view too," Eliza said, "but Sam comes of age soon and he wasn't going to be told what to do."

Judith let her head fall onto the back of the settee. "He left home because of a servant and nobody told me."

"But he didn't murder Grandmother," Flora said.

"No, I believe you may have saved him. Your story matches his and that may be enough to get him out of the cell, for the time being at least. It does mean, however, that someone else did it."

Flora's eyes were wide. "It wasn't me."

"And it wasn't me either." Judith sat up straight in her chair. "I asked you to look into this whole thing. I wouldn't have insisted if I'd been the killer."

"No, unless that's what you wanted me to think." Eliza held Judith's gaze until she turned away. "The problem is, all these lies have made me suspect everyone, including you. After all, you had a strong motive and the opportunity."

"You have to believe me, as much as I disliked Mother, I didn't kill her."

Eliza stood up and walked to the window. "As you saw, while I was waiting for you, I had a flick through this." Eliza held up the notepad from the hall.

"That's private ... it's Frank's."

"So does that mean you haven't looked through it? Or did Frank tell you what he'd found?"

Judith looked from Eliza to Connie. "No ... yes ... I don't know."

"You mean that even now, you can't decide whether to tell us the truth? Please, Judith dear, you need to trust us. We already know that Mr Wilson wanted his job back in London and that the company had withdrawn the offer. What everyone forgot to tell us was the reason why. Is that why Mr Wilson travelled to London on the afternoon of his mother's death? Because he'd found out Mrs Milwood was behind the rejection?"

Judith shook her head. "He didn't know it was Mother, not then. What he told you was true: they wouldn't tell him why he couldn't have the job."

Eliza flicked through Frank's notebook, which was still in her hand. "Frank's very meticulous in his notes. It says here, it was the day before Mrs Milwood's death that he found out what she'd done. Who did he tell? You?"

Judith shifted in her seat.

"We've heard that you and Mr Wilson argued on the Tuesday evening. Was that because you told him the news when he came home from work?"

Judith put her head in her hands, but said nothing.

"I understand this is upsetting, dear, but we need to look at it from the police's point of view. As it stands, I can imagine how tempting it must have been for one of you to poison her. With his mother gone, not only would Mr Wilson get his old job back but the position of managing director as well. He could have gone to London knowing she was already dying; the timing would be perfect. Give his mother the digitalis before she went to bed and then go to London the following day to be well out of the way."

While she'd been talking, Eliza failed to hear the door to the drawing room open and Mr Wilson walk in.

"No, that's not how it happened." Mr Wilson's voice caused Eliza to jump. "I was angry with her, I can't deny that, but I didn't murder her. For all her faults, she was my mother."

"Mr Wilson." Eliza took a deep breath before telling him of Sam's arrest. "If I'm to help him, I need the truth from you."

"Of course. I've been honest with you all along." He took a seat opposite his wife.

"Are you sure? Initially, you lied about being in work on the day of your mother's death and then you didn't tell anyone it was your mother who had blocked your job."

"I told you, it was a mistake..."

Eliza sighed. "The police may accept one mistake, but not two. You found out about the job on the Tuesday, didn't you?"

"I went to London to see if the board would change their minds, but they told me about Mother's intervention and said it was more than their jobs were worth to go against her. She would have had no hesitation in getting rid of people who didn't do what she wanted. If I'd known she was dying, I could have got them to think again."

Eliza nodded. "All right, let's imagine that's true, tell me what you knew about the donation your mother was planning on making to the church. I heard it was for one thousand pounds. That's a lot of money for you to lose from your inheritance and another motive to add to the list."

The colour drained from Mr Wilson's face. "It's not what it seems."

"Then why lie about it?"

Mr Wilson ran a hand across his face. "Because I knew what it would look like. The police could accuse me of murdering Mother for any number of reasons, but I didn't. You must believe me."

Eliza sighed. "You're the third person in this room who's said that in the last half an hour. Why should I? Is there anyone who can verify what you were doing between midnight and midday on the day your mother died?"

Mr Wilson shook his head. "I didn't do anything ... not that would kill her."

"But you did do something?" Eliza raised an eyebrow at him.

"I confronted her about the job and the donation and told her that if she was giving my inheritance away, then there was no point in us staying. I also said that if I couldn't get a job with Moreton Industries, I'd get one elsewhere."

"And what did she say to that?"

Mr Wilson stood up and poured himself a whisky from the decanter on the sideboard. He took a large mouthful. Eliza watched each move but when he failed to respond she glanced at Connie.

"I'm guessing she wasn't very pleased," Connie said.

Eliza opened her mouth to reply, but as she did, she noticed Flora sitting with her eyes focussed on the carpet. "Flora, I get the impression you know about this conversation. What did your grandmother say when your father told her he'd leave with or without a job at Moreton Industries?"

All eyes turned to Flora but she put her head in her hands. "Don't make me tell you."

"Tell them," Mr Wilson said.

Flora's voice was almost inaudible. "Over my dead body."

Eliza gawked at Flora. "Your grandmother said to your father that he would get another job in London *over her dead body*?"

Flora nodded before Eliza walked over to the window.

"All right, so now we're getting somewhere." She turned back to face the room. "I'm guessing that both Flora and Judith overheard that conversation and ever since have lived in fear that Mr Wilson had indeed murdered his mother so they could move back to London. That's one of the reasons for the lies. Am I right?"

When the women remained silent, Eliza walked back to Mr Wilson. "I told you not five minutes ago that your son's being held on suspicion of murder. Are you prepared to let him hang for something you did?"

Mr Wilson's eyes were moist. "I'd take his place if I could, but I swear I didn't touch her. I can't confess to something I didn't do."

Eliza paused and turned back to Judith. "Which leaves us with you. When you overheard that conversation did you take Mrs Milwood's life to save your husband and give your family their lives back?"

Mr Wilson looked at his wife, the strain unmistakable.

"No, it wasn't me. I might have had good reason, but I've told you, I was resigned to the fact she was likely to die sooner or later and was prepared to bide my time."

Eliza put a hand to her forehead and rubbed her eyes. "Please, Judith dear, we're supposed to be telling the truth. Now, you told Mrs Milwood you'd had enough of her dominating your family and that she could keep her money.

You also told her you were prepared to move back to London and get a job yourself."

"Who said...?" Judith's eyes were wide as she turned from Eliza to her husband. "I didn't mean it, I was angry with her. I'd forgotten I'd said it..."

"No, you hadn't. Not only did you tell Mrs Milwood, you told your husband the same thing the morning before the murder. Didn't she, Flora?"

Flora's cheeks turned scarlet.

"No, this is all wrong." Judith was on her feet. "I didn't do it. I wouldn't let my son hang any more than Joseph would."

"Neither of them did it." Flora jumped to her feet and looked first at her mother and then her father. "They both argued with Grandmother but neither would have killed her. They wouldn't. They were going to go to London and leave her here on her own. Why take her life if they were happy to walk away with nothing?"

Connie's forehead creased. "Were they really happy to walk away with nothing? Or has this whole thing been a charade to cover your tracks? Were you so concerned that you took the decision from them?"

Fear was evident in Flora's eyes and she paused before shaking her head. "No, it wasn't me."

Eliza studied each of the suspects. "All right, we're not going to solve anything tonight. I need time to think and I'm sure you do too. From what I can tell the three of you all had a motive and opportunity to murder Mrs Milwood, as did Sam, but each of you deny having anything to do with it. It seems to me you're all afraid that one of the others could be the murderer and that's what's prompted the lies. You're trying to cover up for each other when you actually don't know the truth yourselves."

"But we're all certain it wasn't us," Judith said.

"Then in that case, I suggest it's about time you were all perfectly honest with each other and tried to piece things together yourselves. We'll leave you to it, but you need to remember one thing. As things stand, Sam is the police's main suspect, and so if you want to save him from the gallows you have to be honest. Come along, Connie, I think it's time for dinner. We can see ourselves out."

CHAPTER TWENTY-FIVE

As Tuesday morning drew to a close, Connie popped her head into the dispensary to find Eliza making up the last of her prescriptions.

"Still at it?" she asked with a smile.

"I am, but I'm going as fast as I can. Give me another five minutes."

Connie took a seat alongside the counter. "Have you had any more thoughts on the Wilsons since yesterday evening?"

Eliza attached a label to the bottle she was working on. "I've done nothing else since I left you. What about you?"

"Yes, the same. I can't believe it's come down to this. One of them must have done it, and yet they're still lying even though it could mean Sam goes to the gallows."

Eliza put the stopper back on the bottle in front of her and walked around the counter. "That's the problem. It's also why I don't think any of them did it."

Connie's eyes were wide. "None of them? But I thought we were going to the police this afternoon."

Eliza took a seat next to her friend. "What would we say?

We've no proof that Judith or Mr Wilson committed the murder, or Flora for that matter. That was why I walked away last night."

"But clearly someone did it and if it wasn't them, who else would have the motive or the opportunity?"

"That, my dear Connie, is the all-important question. We urgently need to find the real killer so we can get Sam released and the Wilsons can carry on with their lives."

"Well, who else could it be?"

Eliza groaned as she pushed herself up from the chair. "I've no idea. We're no closer to knowing where the digitalis came from either. I asked Archie if he'd speak to the doctor in Over Moreton to check whether he was missing any, but he told me last night he's not."

"Maybe it was someone from outside the village then. The unlocked front door at the Wilsons' may be more than a coincidence after all."

"If it was, there's no chance of finding out who did it. The killer will be long gone, and what motive would they have? I fear that we've come to a dead end and I can't see a way forward at the moment."

Connie sat in silence for several seconds but then bolted upright. "I'll tell you who we should go and see. Ruby. I don't expect anyone's told her that Sam's back, or that he's been arrested. Someone needs to speak to her."

"You're right. I'll tell you what, why don't you stay for luncheon and then we can take the carriage over to the manor house this afternoon? The inspector should be back in the village tomorrow and we can tell him what we've found out before we do anything else. He may be the fresh pair of eyes we need."

Connie smiled. "I like that idea. It'll be nice to see all the flowers in bloom."

As Eliza and Connie finished their cups of tea, Archie went to arrange the carriage for their afternoon outing.

"It's a lovely day for it," he said, as he walked back into the room to tell them it was ready. "I almost wish I was coming with you."

Eliza chuckled. "I'm sure you'd change your mind after the first five minutes. Listening to women's talk never was one of your things."

"You're right." He held the front door open for them. "Well, enjoy your afternoon, while I make do with my house visits ... and drive carefully!"

"He seems to have settled in well," Connie said as they took their seats and Eliza flicked the reins causing the carriage to move forward.

"He has for now. Everyone's keen to meet him and give him their whole medical history, which takes up a lot of time. I still worry that once he knows everyone he'll be bored."

"He'll be too busy playing bowls by then; people are saying he's got a knack for it."

Eliza rolled her eyes. "He's got a knack for a lot of things, it's more a question of whether he enjoys it. Still, we'll see."

Despite Connie's parasol shading them, the sun had been warm on the journey over and Eliza was grateful to pull into the shade of the manor house when they arrived.

"We'll need to get some water for the horses while we're here."

"I can see to that for you." The butler stepped from the

front door as they climbed from the carriage and signalled to a coachman.

"Thank you." Eliza watched as the horses were led away. "You really are most efficient."

"I'm only doing my job, madam. How may I help?"

Eliza smiled. "You may remember we called last week to speak with one of your servant girls, Ruby. We wondered if we might speak with her again. We're working with the police on a crime in Moreton-on-Thames and she may be able to help."

If the butler remembered their previous visit, or was surprised by this request, he kept it to himself. He stepped to one side before showing them into the drawing room.

"Can I get you some tea while you're waiting, or perhaps some lemonade?"

"Lemonade would be lovely, thank you."

Five minutes later Ruby walked into the drawing room carrying a tray with a jug of cloudy liquid and two glasses.

"Good afternoon, Ruby."

"Mrs Appleton! I wasn't told it was you. Do you have any news?" Ruby's dark eyes twinkled as the sunlight streamed through the large windows.

Eliza waited for her to put the tray down. "Won't you sit down? We'd like to talk to you."

Ruby's eyes darted between the two women. "It's not bad news, is it?"

"Well, first of all, there is good news," Connie said. "Sam's been found safe and well."

A relieved smile formed on Ruby's lips before her face fell. "Why didn't he come and see me then? Was I right that I've upset him?"

"No," Eliza said. "I think I'm safe in saying that he loves you very much. The problem is that as soon as he arrived back in Moreton-on-Thames, he was arrested for the murder of Mrs Milwood."

Eliza paused as Ruby gasped.

"No, he couldn't have. He wouldn't. He promised me."

Eliza flicked her eyes towards Connie before turning back to Ruby. "What did he promise you?"

Ruby hesitated. "That ... that he wouldn't do anything stupid."

"Such as?"

When there was no response, Connie interrupted. "It's the police who arrested him. We suspect he's innocent and want to help. If you have any information that could help, please tell us."

"Even if you think it may incriminate him," Eliza added as Ruby hesitated.

With tears welling in her eyes, Ruby's voice was a whisper. "He wouldn't have used them."

"You knew he had the bottles of medicine from Dr Thomson's surgery?"

Ruby nodded. "He said he'd found them and joked about using them on his grandmother, but I made him promise that he wouldn't. I told him I'd rather wait until we could be together than see him hang."

"And did he promise?"

With tears now rolling down her cheeks, Ruby nodded. "Yes. He even said he wouldn't know what to do with them and would take them straight back to the surgery."

"Is that why he went to Moreton-on-Thames on the afternoon of Mrs Milwood's death? To take the bottles back?"

"That's what he told me, but he wanted to speak to her as well. He promised me he wouldn't hurt her."

"Had he been to Moreton the day before too?"

Ruby wiped her eyes with her handkerchief. "I don't think so. He came to see me on the Tuesday evening when I had a break. He'd sometimes wait for me by the gate in case I could sneak out, and he said he was going straight back to his room that evening."

"What time was he here on the Tuesday?" Connie asked.

Ruby shrugged. "Between about half past seven and eight o'clock, I would say, before the family were ready to dine."

"That's good," Eliza said. "The more we can place him here, the less likelihood there is of him being at his grandmother's house. His landlady said he was at the house at ten o'clock when she locked up for the night."

Ruby nodded again. "Thank goodness for that."

Eliza smiled. "The only problem is that we need to find the person who did poison Mrs Milwood. It's our best chance of getting him released. What can you tell us about his sister, Flora?"

"Flora? You don't think she did it, do you?"

"At this point, we have to suspect everyone," Eliza said. "It seems she's something of a loner."

"She is since she moved here, but Sam said how much she had changed. She had a large circle of friends in London and she didn't want to mix with the girls down here when they first moved. Sam said she thought they were beneath her."

"Cheeky madam." Connie's words caused Eliza to laugh.

"It's a good job Mrs Appleton didn't know about that yesterday when we were talking to her."

"She has some strange ideas," Ruby said. "She's

determined to get back to London and study to be a doctor. She talks about nothing else."

"Is she close to Sam?" Eliza asked.

Ruby shrugged. "Not particularly."

"Did you know she encouraged Sam to take the bottles from the surgery and told him what to do with them?"

Ruby's eyes grew wide. "She was behind it? Trying to get Sam to do her dirty work. How could she?"

"We can't say that for certain, so please don't go around repeating it. It's quite an accusation to suggest she would send her brother to the gallows just because she wanted to study medicine. It's not exactly the philosophy behind being a doctor."

Ruby shuddered. "Maybe not, but like I said, she's desperate to get back to London."

Eliza stood up and paced the room. "I need to think about this."

The room fell silent, each with their own thoughts before Connie spoke.

"When you look at it, poor Mrs Milwood didn't stand a chance, did she? Everyone in the family had a reason for wanting her dead, and she did nothing to endear herself to any of them. It's a good job she had a friend in Mrs Harris."

For the first time in a week, Ruby laughed. "Who told you that?"

"Who told me what? That everyone wanted her dead?"

"No, that she was friendly with Mrs Harris. Cook disliked her as much as everyone else."

Connie turned to Eliza as her friend rounded on Ruby.

"Why did Cook dislike her?"

Ruby shrugged. "Nothing in particular, but Mrs Milwood

was always complaining. She didn't like the food, the menus, the grocery bills. Cook would call Mrs Milwood every name under the sun when it was just the two of us."

Connie looked at Eliza. "So why would she tell us she was the only one who got along with her?"

"That, my dear Mrs Appleton, is a good question. Tell me, Ruby, we've heard that Cook had a friend who she visits on her afternoon off. You wouldn't happen to know who it is, would you?"

Ruby giggled. "She has a man friend."

"Mrs Harris does?" Connie put a hand to her mouth. "Well I never! I expect that's why she wouldn't tell anyone. She'd be frightened of causing a scandal."

"How long has she known him?" Eliza asked.

Ruby puffed out her cheeks. "I can't say for certain, she never confided in me. I only know what I've heard since I moved here."

"And what have you heard?"

"His name's Mr Robins and he works as a gardener in one of the bigger houses in Over Moreton. But..." Ruby paused for effect "...word has it he's asked her to marry him."

"Really?" Connie's eyes lit up but Eliza cut across the conversation.

"How would that work in terms of living arrangements?"

"That's the thing," Ruby said. "The rumour is that there's a post for a new cook where Mr Robins works and they want to get married so they can get the married couple's quarters."

"It must be a step up from working for the Wilsons," Connie said.

"Oh, it is. The only thing that makes me wonder if the rumours are true is the fact she hasn't moved jobs yet. I first heard about it last month and would have expected her to have moved by now if it were true."

"Ruby." Eliza beamed at the girl in front of her. "You have no idea how helpful you've been. I think the next thing Mrs Appleton and I need to do is go to this house and see if indeed there is a position for a new cook ... and whether Mrs Harris has been offered the post." She handed Ruby a notepad for her to write down the address. "We'll then report to the police inspector tomorrow to see what he makes of it all."

With her notebook back in her bag, Eliza turned to Connie. "Come along, Mrs Appleton, we've some investigating to do."

CHAPTER TWENTY-SIX

The carriage carrying Eliza and Connie arrived back on the main street of Over Moreton within five minutes of leaving the manor, and Eliza guided the horses down a secluded cul-de-sac on her left-hand side.

"I've never been down here." Eliza retrieved the notebook from her bag. "We're looking for 'Ballyhoe'. Have you any idea which one it is?"

"No, I've never been down here either. It looks like the sort of place you only visit if you need to."

"I'd better drive slowly then. It's difficult to see the houses behind all those trees."

They made their way past several houses before Eliza brought the horses to a standstill alongside a hedge in front of one of the houses.

"Was that Mrs Harris I saw?"

Connie turned back towards the gate. "I didn't notice."

Eliza handed Connie the reins and climbed down from the carriage before creeping back to the gates at the front of the house. She peered up the front drive as Connie joined her.

"What is it?"

Eliza nodded towards the garden. "Don't let them see you, but would you say that's Mr Robins?"

Connie poked her head round the gatepost. "I should say so, but why the secrecy? I thought we were here to talk to him."

Eliza put a finger to her lips and looked again into the garden. "Come on, we've got to go." Grabbing Connie by the hand, she pulled her back to the carriage before turning it around and heading back towards Moreton-on-Thames.

"Are you going to tell me what's going on?" Connie asked as the horses trotted out of Over Moreton.

"We need to get to the Wilsons' before Mrs Harris gets back."

Connie's forehead creased. "What's the rush? I imagine she'll be out all evening."

"I wouldn't be so sure. It looked to me as if she was about to leave. I thought her day off was Wednesday, but it's only Tuesday today. Why's she here?"

Connie's frown deepened. "What's that got to do with Mrs Milwood's death? That was nearly two weeks ago and Judith may have let her change her days."

"Let's go and ask her, shall we?" Eliza flicked the reins on the carriage to speed up the horses. "We need to speak to Judith while Mrs Harris is out ... and please, let me do the talking ... and agree with everything I say."

"Don't I always!"

·   ·   ·

Judith's eyes were red as she opened the door to Eliza and Connie five minutes later.

"I didn't think you'd be back so soon."

Eliza breezed past her into the hall. "I'm sorry to trouble you, my dear, but I'm here on an errand. I've a very efficient cook who's preparing a stew for tomorrow's dinner. The problem is she's run out of herbs to put in it. Would you mind if we took some of yours? I'll return them of course once she can get to the shop."

Connie stared at Eliza, her mouth open.

"The shop will still be open," Judith said.

"No, it's not. We called earlier but they've closed early for the day. No idea why."

"How strange," Judith said. "They usually close on a Wednesday afternoon."

"That's what we thought," Eliza said. "Would you mind asking Mrs Harris for me?"

Connie was about to open her mouth but closed it again when Eliza glared at her.

"You'd better come through to the kitchen then," Judith said. "I'd hoped it was Sam at the door when I opened it, or at least that you'd come to tell me you've got him out of the police cell."

Eliza sighed. "I'm sorry, not yet, but we're working on it."

Judith held open the kitchen door, but as they walked in, the room was empty.

"Where is Mrs Harris?" Judith popped her head into the pantry.

"Is it her afternoon off?" Eliza asked.

"No, she always has Wednesdays off." Judith walked to

the back door and looked out into the garden. "Mrs Harris, are you out there?"

"Are we all mistaken, and it's really Wednesday?" Eliza said. "First the shop's closed and then Mrs Harris is missing." She looked at Connie. "Have we been working so hard we've forgotten what day it is?"

"I'm sure she won't be far away." Judith ignored Eliza's mirth. "Anyway, let's see what she's got in the cupboard."

Judith took down several bottles and lined them up on the worktop.

"Here we are, comfrey. That's what we need." Eliza held up the bottle. "Oh, what a shame, there isn't much left. Perhaps I could take a pinch." She reached into her bag and pulled out a clean handkerchief.

"We've more growing in the garden if you want to take some fresh," Judith said. "I was upstairs one afternoon a couple of weeks ago and saw Mrs Harris picking some."

"If you have enough that would be delightful. We need to plant our own kitchen garden in the next few weeks. I've been a bit preoccupied..."

Judith led them into the garden and took the path leading to the back wall. "She came up here for them."

Eliza was halfway down the path when Mrs Harris' voice pierced the air. "What's going on out here?"

"There you are." Judith turned and walked back to the house. "I didn't think you'd gone far. Mrs Thomson's looking to borrow some comfrey, but there wasn't much in the cupboard. I said she could take a few fresh leaves."

"Well, you're going to the wrong place. The comfrey's here, near the back door for easy access." Mrs Harris moved to the patch of plants with elongated leaves and pulled out a few stalks.

Eliza studied the back of the garden before returning to the house, her brow creased.

"Here you are, will that be enough?" Cook thrust a bunch of leaves towards Eliza as she approached the back door.

"Yes, I'm sure that's more than enough, thank you so much. I'll get these to Cook now so as not to slow her down any further." She turned once more to study the back of the garden.

"You're very fortunate having such a well-stocked garden," Eliza said to Judith as they reached the front door. "Do you have a gardener?"

Judith shook her head. "We used to, but it was something else Mother stopped. I try to keep it tidy and Cook tends to the herbs. She knows more about it than me."

"And you keep all the herbs in that plot near the back door?"

"Yes, I think so. It makes it easier for Cook."

After saying their farewells, Eliza and Connie walked back to the carriage they'd left round the corner from the Wilsons'.

"What was all that about?" Connie asked. "You knew Mrs Harris was out, and we didn't even go to the shop to see if it was open."

Eliza grinned. "Forgive me, they were just a couple of white lies. I'm still puzzling over where the digitalis came from and so I wanted a sample of the comfrey from the kitchen. It looks very much like the foxglove plant and could easily be switched."

The frown on Connie's face didn't change. "And why's that important?"

"Because, my dear Connie, the foxglove is the source of our medicinal digitalis."

"Oh, of course." Connie rolled her eyes and climbed into the carriage. She was about to take her seat when Eliza walked straight past her. "Where are you going?"

Eliza stopped and stared at her. "What are you doing in there? Come along, we're going to pay Mrs Petty a visit."

"Mrs Petty? What on earth for?"

"Because she gave the police some rather useful information and we've never followed it up with her. I also want to look in her garden."

Eliza strode towards the house and knocked on the door before Connie had the chance to ask any questions.

"Can you introduce us?" Eliza asked as Connie joined her. "I've never met the woman."

"I've heard a lot about you," Mrs Petty said to Eliza once the introductions were over. "I wondered when you'd be round. Come on in, I've got the kettle on."

"Do you live here alone?" Eliza asked.

"I do. I lost my dear husband many years ago and never got around to finding another."

"Children?"

"No. I live alone and keep myself to myself." The silence that followed was abrupt and Eliza changed the subject.

"The house is in a grand spot though. I expect you can watch most of the village from here and the comings and goings of those travelling to Over Moreton."

"It keeps me occupied." There was a glint in the old woman's eye.

"Tell me," Eliza said, "did you see Mrs Harris leave the village about an hour ago?"

"It was probably closer to two hours. A gentleman came to pick her up in a carriage, not a man I know."

"And he brought her back?"

"Not more than a quarter of an hour ago, I would say. Do you think it has anything to do with Mrs Milwood's death?"

Eliza grinned. "I can see you don't sit idle while you're here. I always say it's important to keep your mind active. To answer your question, I'm not sure. We've just called at the Wilsons' to speak to Mrs Harris and were surprised to find her out, with it being a Tuesday, you understand. Did you often see her leave the village when she should be working?"

"Now you mention it, I have noticed it recently. I would say it started about a month ago. The first once or twice she slipped out when Mrs Wilson took Mrs Milwood for her walk, but since *the incident*, she seems to disappear whether Mrs Wilson is out or not."

"Is it always the same man who collects her and brings her back?"

"Always..."

"How long has she been widowed?" Connie asked.

Despite the fact she was in her own house, Mrs Petty glanced over both shoulders and lowered her voice. "She's never been married. She told me once she bought a cheap ring and made herself a 'Mrs' to make herself more respectable. I ask you. Not that it made any difference, if you see her with this new gentleman friend. She sits there in the carriage thinking she's Lady Muck. She should be ashamed of herself."

"Can I take it you don't have a lot of time for her?"

"Not got much time for any of them to be honest. Mrs

Milwood was a right one, another one who thought she was a cut above the rest of us. She'd look straight through you if she passed you in the street. Mrs Wilson would smile, but she couldn't stop to talk."

Eliza rummaged in her bag and pulled out her notebook. "You told the police you heard Mr and Mrs Wilson arguing the day before Mrs Milwood was found dead. Rather than it being his wife he was arguing with, could Mr Wilson have been arguing with his mother?"

Mrs Petty cocked her head to one side. "I suppose so, although what man would speak to his mother like that?"

"I presume you were out in the garden when you heard them?"

Mrs Petty's eyes twinkled again. "Early evening is always an entertaining time to go into the garden, you never know what you might learn."

"I can see we should have spoken to you sooner," Eliza said. "Would you mind taking us into the garden now so we can take a look at how close you are to the Wilsons' house?"

Connie shrugged at Eliza as they followed Mrs Petty into the garden.

"It's a good long garden that runs right across the back of the Wilsons' garden." Mrs Petty gestured to the border running down the left-hand side of the lawn. "I've been putting some chrysanthemums in the side that joins their land."

Eliza took her time strolling along the border, occasionally stopping to examine a plant. When she reached the back corner, she stopped and crouched down to peer through the fence.

"Is everything all right?" Connie asked as she and Mrs Petty approached her.

Eliza put a smile on her face as she stood up. "Yes, everything's fine. You have some lovely plants, Mrs Petty."

"You can hear quite a lot from here if anyone raises their voice, especially the men. They always talk so loud."

"Yes, of course, it's a shame women don't speak up more." Eliza peered back over the fence. "Is that the drawing room at the far corner of the house?"

"It is, and can you see they have the windows open? It's often difficult not to overhear."

Eliza smiled. "Still, it's a good twenty or thirty feet away. Is there a chance you mistook Mrs Wilson for Mrs Milwood the day before the murder?"

"Now I think about it, I suppose it is possible. It was Mr Wilson's voice that was most clear. There's no mistaking him ... or Mr Hewitt when he called either."

"Mr Hewitt? Did you overhear the conversation about the donation to the church?"

"Ah, is that what it was about. I missed the start of it and they had me confused. It all makes sense now."

It was another ten minutes before they extricated themselves from Mrs Petty's front porch and as Connie sank into the carriage, the church bells struck five o'clock.

"Good grief, is that the time?" Connie said. "I need to get my dinner on."

"Yes..." Eliza barely heard Connie's words. "I need to go back to Over Moreton. Do you want me to take you home or will you come with me?"

"Now?" Connie's eyes were wide. "What's so important that it can't wait until tomorrow?"

"I need to check Ruby's story about that vacancy for a cook."

Connie let out a loud sigh. "You could have done that while we were there but you dashed off here instead."

"I'm sorry, but it had to be like that." She flicked the reins of the carriage. "I promise I'll be quick."

CHAPTER TWENTY-SEVEN

Early the following morning Eliza and Archie were sitting at the breakfast table. He was reading the morning paper, but she was too preoccupied to do anything other than scribble a few final notes into her notepad.

"Don't you want that?" Archie nodded at the last piece of toast in the rack.

"I couldn't eat a thing at the moment. I need to get to the police station as soon as is polite."

Archie scraped butter over the toast. "Are you sure you know who the culprit is?"

Eliza stood up. "I think so, but I need to go through the evidence with the inspector in case I'm wrong."

"You had your head in those medical books for long enough last night and we talked through the details of the poisoning, again. You know as well as I do that you don't think you're wrong. Does that mean you won't tell me who our poisoner is?"

"Not yet. Please indulge me a little longer." She took a

deep breath and stared at the clock. "Is it too early to go to the police station?"

"It's not eight o'clock yet. If the inspector's travelling from London, I'm sure he won't arrive before ten."

"No, you're right. Shall I walk round there and ask the sergeant to send him here when he arrives? No, that won't do. He'll want to know what's going on, but I need to tell the inspector first."

Archie folded his newspaper. "The first patient won't be here for another half an hour, why don't I walk up there and ask Sergeant Cooper to pass on your message?"

"Oh, will you? I knew there was a reason I didn't want to tell you who the murderer is. What you don't know, you can't talk about."

Archie sighed and pushed himself up from the table. "Anything to stop you worrying and get you doing some work this morning."

As the morning wore on, it felt as if she hadn't gone more than five minutes without looking at the clock. Finally, at half past ten, Inspector Adams walked into the dispensary.

"Inspector!" Eliza's eyes lit up before she remembered the patient sitting in the corner of the room. "I'm almost finished here, I just need to get this prescription made up. Can you give me five minutes and I'll be with you?"

Eliza felt the inspector's dark, penetrating eyes watching her as she worked on the lotion she was preparing. When it was ready and bottled up, she handed it to the patient and walked him to the door, closing it behind him.

"Thank you for coming, Inspector," she said. "I know it's

quite irregular, but I was keen to speak to you as soon as possible."

The inspector nodded. "I'm charmed, I'm sure, but Sergeant Cooper has filled me in on the details."

"Oh dear, I was afraid of that." Eliza walked to the window. "Please don't believe everything he's told you. They've arrested the wrong man."

The inspector's smile faded. "They told me it was all wrapped up. The young man in the cell disappeared on the day of his grandmother's death only to turn up a week later to admit he'd visited her on the day she died. He has also admitted to taking a substantial amount of money from her."

Eliza's face paled. "The money was family money and hasn't officially been reported as stolen, but the point is, he's not our poisoner. Have you spoken to him? Or charged him?"

"Not yet, I thought I'd better come here first."

"Thank goodness for that. Please, can I offer you some tea and I'll take you through the evidence? I only put the final pieces together last night, and I wanted to get your expert opinion on it before I told anyone else."

The inspector nodded and followed her into the house where she ordered tea before going into the drawing room.

"So you think Samuel Wilson is innocent of murder?" Inspector Adams said once the tea had been delivered. "If he is, why has he remained in custody for two days?"

Eliza sighed. "He'd been arrested before I found out he was back from London. I went to see him as soon as I could, but I must admit, although I don't think he's guilty, the evidence against him is strong."

"So why do you believe he's innocent?"

Eliza shrugged. "It probably sounds silly but I suppose

you could call it intuition. My friend Mrs Appleton and I spoke to him for quite some time and you could tell in his eyes he had no idea what was happening. He gave us a detailed account of the afternoon of the murder, and of the previous evening, which all the relevant people have since confirmed. For reasons that I'll go into later, I'm of the opinion that Mrs Milwood was poisoned the previous evening, but Sam's landlady and a young lady he was walking out with have both confirmed he was in Over Moreton at the time in question."

"Did you tell this to the sergeant?"

Eliza turned her attention to the tea. "I only confirmed some of the details late yesterday and so haven't had time."

"Hmm." The inspector studied her. "So, are you going to tell me who did poison Mrs Milwood?"

It took over an hour to go through all the details in her notebook and when she finally closed it, the inspector sat back in his chair.

"I clearly underestimated you, you've done well."

Eliza struggled to suppress a smile. "Have I left any gaps?"

"Not that I can see, other than getting a confession. We need to get everyone together and go through the evidence. Once the suspect realises what we know, they usually confess."

Eliza nodded. "That makes sense."

"I'll tell Sergeant Cooper to be at the Wilsons' house for three o'clock this afternoon with Sam and Constable Jenkins. I'll call on everyone else involved; it might take my authority to get them all there. Will that suit you?"

Eliza let out a deep breath. "I think so. Dr Thomson should be free by then and I'll tell Mrs Appleton too."

. . .

As the church bells struck three o'clock, Judith opened the front door to Eliza, Connie and Archie.

"What on earth's going on?" Judith asked as she closed the door behind them. "There are more people in the drawing room than I've had for many a year but nobody will tell me why."

"Is the inspector here?" Eliza asked.

At that moment there was another knock on the front door and Judith opened it to find the inspector standing alongside Sam, who was firmly handcuffed to Sergeant Cooper.

"Sam!" She threw her arms around her son but the sergeant moved to keep them apart.

"That's enough, please, Mrs Wilson. Your son's in police custody and is only here to listen to what the inspector has to say."

"Is Constable Jenkins watching over everyone who's here?" Inspector Adams asked.

"He was when I left," Judith said. "Will someone please tell me what's happening?"

Inspector Adams looked down at her. "We have enough information to identify the person who murdered Mrs Milwood."

Judith's eyes were wide as she turned to Eliza. "Do you know about this?"

"Why didn't you tell me?" Connie caught hold of Eliza's arm. "Has anyone been arrested?"

"Not yet." Eliza gave an apologetic smile.

"All in good time," Inspector Adams said. "Shall we go through? I hope I'm right in assuming everyone else is here."

Judith glared at the inspector. "As I've no idea who you've

invited, I'll let you answer that for yourself." She led them to the drawing room and knocked on the door where Constable Jenkins had taken up his position. He held the door open and Eliza glanced around the room to check who was present. Ruby's face lit up as Sam walked in but the smile faded when she noticed the handcuffs tying him to Sergeant Cooper. Mrs Harris sat to Ruby's left at the back of the room.

Next to them, on chairs that had been brought in from the dining room, was the vicar, along with Mr Hewitt and Mrs Petty. Connie and Archie took the nearest of the empty dining chairs and sat down, while Eliza remained standing. She acknowledged Mr Wilson, who was sitting on the settee with Flora and Frank.

"I think there's one missing," Inspector Adams said. "Has anyone seen Mr Robins?"

Mrs Harris' mouth fell open, but as soon as she noticed Eliza staring at her she closed it again.

"Constable, go and see if he's outside," the inspector said. "Sergeant, you take the door."

Sergeant Cooper looked down at his handcuffed wrist and pulled Sam over to the door with him.

No sooner had Constable Jenkins left the house than he returned with a rosy-cheeked Mr Robins.

"There you are," Inspector Adams said. "Take a seat, if you don't mind, and we can begin."

Eliza watched as a hesitant Mr Robins took the seat furthest away from Mrs Harris.

"Very good." The inspector nodded to no one in particular. "Now you're all here, I imagine you're wondering why I called you together at such short notice."

"My employers aren't happy that I've had to take the

afternoon off." Mr Robins' comment prompted several of the men to agree with him.

"Gentlemen, please, I'll write to your employers to offer my thanks once this meeting is over. In the meantime I'm sure none of you need reminding that two weeks ago today, Mrs Milwood was found poisoned in her own bed. Ever since, we've been searching for her killer."

"That doesn't explain why I'm here," Mr Robins said. "I didn't even know the woman."

The inspector fixed him with a piercing gaze before glancing around the room. "I don't suppose you know many of the people here, either. For what it's worth, these are the family and acquaintances of the late Mrs Milwood; everyone, this is Mr Robins and his presence here will be revealed in due course. Now, as I was about to say, thanks to Mrs Thomson, we can now identify our killer."

The sound of gasps around the room stopped the inspector momentarily, although whether it was because the killer had been identified or more specifically because she was the one who had done the identifying, Eliza couldn't be sure.

"From the start this has been a most unusual inquiry," the inspector continued. "Often we struggle to find suspects with both a motive and the opportunity to commit the crime. In this case, however, Mrs Milwood was so unpopular, we had too many suspects.

"First there was Mrs Wilson." He stopped and stared at Judith, who had perched on the arm of the settee alongside her husband. "You were in charge of Mrs Milwood's care and were the one who found the body on the afternoon of Wednesday the thirteenth of June."

Judith nodded solemnly.

"As things were, almost everyone knew that Mrs Milwood made your life a misery and she caused many arguments between yourself and Mr Wilson. You were desperate to go back to London but Mrs Milwood was equally determined to keep you here. Firstly, she told Mr Wilson she had a weak heart and when that failed to weaken his resolve, she threatened to stop his inheritance. Isn't that right, Mr Wilson?"

Mr Wilson squirmed in his seat as the inspector paused for effect.

"It must have been tempting, in the middle of the night when everyone else was sleeping, to sneak into her room and slip some poison into the water she kept by the bedside."

"But I didn't. Eliza, tell him..." Judith's eyes were wide. "We've been over this."

The inspector held up his hands. "You have indeed, Mrs Wilson, but as I said, our problem's been that Mrs Milwood upset many people who could have killed her. And so the question is, if you didn't poison her, who else had the motive and opportunity?" The inspector scanned the room until his eyes rested on Mr Wilson. "Your husband, perhaps. You couldn't be sure, could you?"

Judith's gaze fell to her lap while the eyes of the rest of the room turned to Mr Wilson.

"She was my mother. Of course I didn't murder her."

"That she may have been, sir, but the fact is, she was intent on ruining your life. I understand that before her death, she stopped you from going back to your old job in the family business."

"I wouldn't have killed her just for that."

Inspector Adams studied Mr Wilson. "Maybe not, but

hadn't you also recently learned she planned on leaving a sizeable part of your inheritance to the church? The inheritance she was blackmailing you with? Isn't that right, Mr Hewitt?"

Mr Hewitt sat up straight. "Well, I'm sure I know nothing of blackmail..."

"But you knew of the bequest Mrs Milwood was leaving for the repairs to the bell tower?"

Mr Hewitt shifted uncomfortably. "She'd mentioned it."

"And what did you think when she told you she'd changed her mind and had arranged for her solicitor to call later in the week?"

Mr Hewitt's mouth opened and closed as he turned to the vicar.

"You called here on the Tuesday evening before she died, did you not?" Inspector Adams asked.

"I did, but I wasn't certain she was changing her plans. She said she needed to confirm it."

"Are you sure?" Inspector Adams asked. "We have a witness who overheard you pleading with Mrs Milwood not to forsake the church. Why would you do that when she was leaving you such a generous legacy? Being denied one thousand pounds for a building you love sounds like an excellent motive for murder if you ask me, and you had the opportunity."

"This is preposterous..."

"Inspector Adams!" The vicar's face was red. "Mr Hewitt's a God-fearing man, he'd never dream of harming anyone. I doubt any man would murder someone because of a building."

A smirk crossed the inspector's face. "Your faith in

mankind is touching, Vicar, but sadly not all men share your virtues."

He turned back to Mr Wilson. "Unfortunately, you were unaware that your mother had changed her mind about the donation. You'd overheard her talking about it to Mr Hewitt and she'd mentioned that her solicitor was calling, but you thought it was to add the legacy not remove it. Were you so determined to stop her giving money to the church that you were prepared to take her life for it? It must have come as quite a shock when you read the final copy of the will."

"No, of course I wasn't."

"Well, was it because you'd found out it was your mother who'd prevented your move back to London? You had a wife and daughter who were desperate to go back there and yet you couldn't support them if you left here because your mother wouldn't give you any money or allow you back into your well-paid job. What sort of man has no control over his family?"

Mr Wilson stared at the inspector, his face white. "We were going whether she gave us the money or not. We wanted our lives back."

"A commendable attitude," the inspector continued, "but how much easier would it have been if your mother had met with an accident before she had the chance to pass her money to Mr Hewitt? Then you could have returned to London to head up the family business, hope no one suspected foul play and live happily ever after."

Mr Wilson shook his head. "No. It wasn't like that, I tried to talk to her..."

"And it was a rather heated conversation, by all accounts, wasn't it? We have witnesses who heard Mrs Milwood say that you'd only go back to London over 'her dead body'. When she was found dead less than a day later, you can't deny it looked suspicious."

"I didn't do it." Mr Wilson was on his feet. "Anyone in this room could have slipped some poison into her food. What about Mrs Harris? She prepared all her food, who'd be better placed...?"

"Don't you go blaming me, Mr Wilson." Mrs Harris was also on her feet. "I've been a loyal cook to Mrs Milwood for many a year; I wouldn't dream of doing anything like that. Besides, I don't even know what killed her."

"That's enough." Inspector Adams raised his hands. "Both of you sit down." He paused to stare at everyone in the room.

"The thing is, although Mr Hewitt had a theoretical motive for murdering Mrs Milwood, Mr and Mrs Wilson were the prime suspects and not without reason. That was until their son Samuel turned up in Moreton-on-Thames."

All eyes turned to Sam, who remained handcuffed to Sergeant Cooper.

"Here was a young man who had a lot to be angry with his grandmother about. Unbeknownst to anyone, for several months prior to Mrs Milwood's death, Sam had been walking out with the family's then housemaid Ruby. Unfortunately for the young couple, Mrs Milwood found out about their relationship and decided it was an unsuitable match. She dismissed Ruby from her role here and arranged a position for her at the manor house, over two miles away. This clearly made it difficult for the couple to meet, and although it didn't stop their relationship, they were both aware of Mrs Milwood's threat to deny Sam his inheritance if she found out.

"Not unnaturally, Sam was angry and went to see his grandmother on the afternoon she died. He then promptly disappeared from Moreton without a word to his employer, landlady or indeed Ruby, about where he was going.

"Even before he returned, there were some who saw this as a sign of guilt, but there is one major problem. Sam isn't guilty, in the same way that his parents and Mr Hewitt are not guilty."

Everyone in the room gasped but Inspector Adams addressed Sergeant Cooper.

"Sergeant, please release Samuel Wilson from the handcuffs."

With a look of indignation, the sergeant held out his hand to Constable Jenkins. The constable hesitated until a glare from Inspector Adams forced him to hand over the key.

"Go and sit down, lad," the inspector said. "Now, Mrs Thomson, would you care to explain why the four suspects are innocent."

CHAPTER TWENTY-EIGHT

E liza coughed to clear her throat as she stepped in front of the fireplace to address everyone.

"Thank you, Inspector. As most of you know, Mrs Appleton and I have been helping the police, but from the beginning there were two things about this murder that didn't make sense. The first was the source of the poison given to Mrs Milwood and the second was the time it was administered.

"We know she died because of an overdose of the drug digitalis; we also know that when taken by mouth, digitalis has a slow onset of action. That means that if Mrs Milwood died between half past one and two o'clock in the afternoon, as she did, then we would expect the fatal dose to have been given in the middle of the night. The problem is, if the drug had been administered at that time, the sickness Mrs Milwood reported at half past eleven the next morning would have been too late."

Eliza paused and studied those in the room. "That gave me one fundamental question. Why did Mrs Milwood die so quickly after she'd reported the sickness? This has puzzled me ever since the inquest, but it was only when I found the source of the digitalis that the other pieces of the puzzle fell into place.

"For most of this investigation, I'd assumed the murderer had used digitalis taken either from our surgery or the one in Over Moreton, however, neither Dr Thomson nor Dr Wark had reported any missing. It was only yesterday afternoon I realised my error.

"Not only is digitalis commonly found in doctors' surgeries, it's also present in most gardens. You perhaps know it as the common foxglove, an attractive plant with tall spikes of purple flowers. These plants are incredibly poisonous and at this time of year it's easy to extract the poison, if you know what you're doing. All you'd need would be a quantity of strong alcohol ... like gin, for example, and then you'd boil the leaves in it. Within hours you'd have a home-made tincture of digitalis."

Eliza cast her eyes around the room to check that her audience understood. Reassured that they did, she continued.

"It isn't without its problems though. With a home-made version, it's hard to get the dose right and this set me thinking. What if the initial attempt to poison Mrs Milwood failed? Perhaps a few drops of the tincture were slipped into her bedtime drink but when she woke feeling none the worse for it, our poisoner panicked. She wasn't supposed to wake up. The amount of tincture needed to be increased.

"Giving a second dose could explain our dilemma. The first dose was too low to cause any nausea, but the drug would still have been in the body when the second was given. The second dose was enough to cause the sickness, but because by this time some digitalis had been in Mrs Milwood's system for over twelve hours, it hastened her death."

Eliza once again studied those in the room. A couple offered a degree of interest while others stared at her, confusion on their faces. It was those who refused to acknowledge her who held her interest.

"So, this brings us back to our suspects. Because of the timing of the doses, the suspects needed alibis not only for the night before Mrs Milwood's death, but for early on the Wednesday morning as well. We know Mr Hewitt called here on the Tuesday evening, but we can eliminate him from the list of suspects because there's no evidence he was here on Wednesday morning when the fatal dose was administered."

Eliza allowed herself a smile when the vicar placed a reassuring hand on Mr Hewitt's shoulder.

"We can also eliminate Sam Wilson for similar reasons. Since Ruby began work at the manor house, Sam had taken a room in Over Moreton. We have several witnesses who confirmed he was in Over Moreton on the Tuesday evening and that he was in work by eight o'clock on the Wednesday morning. Even if he'd slipped the tincture into Mrs Milwood's bedtime drink, the fact he was in work the next morning, before his grandmother was out of bed, tells us he would have had no idea the first dose had failed. It also means he wouldn't have been at the house to administer the second dose."

"What if he had an accomplice?" Constable Jenkins' face twisted as he spoke.

"That's a good question, Constable, but the fact is Sam Wilson wasn't in Moreton-on-Thames to deliver either dose of the digitalis and wouldn't have been able to advise on the administration of the second fatal dose. Besides, if he'd slipped the poison into the drinks before he disappeared to London, why would he come back? No, someone else had to have done it, and that someone is in this room."

Eliza once again scanned the room, letting her gaze rest on those refusing to acknowledge her.

"So, let's consider the facts. On the night before Mrs Milwood died, and then again first thing the following morning, there were five other people in the house. Mr and Mrs Wilson, of course, Frank, Flora and the cook, Mrs Harris.

"If we assume the murderer was working alone, both Mr Wilson and Frank have alibis for the Wednesday morning as both left the house at their usual time and have been confirmed as being in work before Mrs Milwood was out of bed. So, that leaves the ladies.

"We know Mrs Wilson put Mrs Milwood to bed the night before she died and took her a coffee the following morning before helping her out of bed. We also know that Mrs Harris prepared the evening meal and was still in the kitchen to help Mrs Wilson with Mrs Milwood's nightcap. She clearly also made breakfast the following morning."

"Don't go blaming me." Cook's eyes shifted around the room. "I had nothing to do with it. Minding my own business I was."

"Thank you, Mrs Harris. I'm sure we'll come back to you in a moment. First, I want to consider young Flora here." She gestured to the settee on her right. "She may only be a young girl but she's determined to go back to London and study medicine at university. She's been preparing by reading a selection of medical textbooks in her room and I would suggest that if anyone knows about the toxic effects of the foxglove plant, it's her."

"But ... that's nonsense," Flora said. "I didn't even see Grandmother that morning. I'd taken breakfast and gone back to my room before she was out of bed."

"A few drops of tincture in a cup that was already set on the table for her might have been all that was needed. Then you'd have been out of the way and beyond suspicion."

"That's a ludicrous suggestion, which you'd realise if you knew anything about medicine. A tincture of digitalis would leave a horribly bitter taste in the mouth, one that would certainly not be masked by a cup of tea. I would have been much more inventive if I'd wanted to poison her."

Eliza looked down at the young woman. "You've clearly done your reading. You're right, a cup of tea wouldn't have a strong enough taste to mask the digitalis. A strong cup of coffee, on the other hand, would be, especially if someone had sweetened it with an extra spoonful of sugar."

Eliza's eyes flicked between Judith and Mrs Harris. "Mrs Wilson told us she had taken a cup of coffee up to Mrs Milwood at around eight o'clock on the morning of her death, shortly before she got out of bed. This was something she did every morning, but on the day in question, Mrs Milwood didn't finish it and complained it had been over-sweetened. Why would that be, Mrs Harris? You prepared that cup of coffee, didn't you?"

"I made it as I always do. Anyone could have put an extra spoonful of sugar in it, or some poison. I didn't see it once it left the kitchen."

Eliza continued as if she hadn't heard her. "You also had a hand in preparing Mrs Milwood's nightcap of brandy the night before. You added what Mrs Wilson thought was a dash of water but rather than using water from the tap, which was your usual practice, you used a clear liquid from a jug on the kitchen counter. I'd like to suggest that rather than it being water, it was in fact a tincture of digitalis you'd made from one of the bottles of gin in the pantry."

"I don't know what you're talking about."

"Oh, but I think you do," Eliza said. "The problem was, Mrs Milwood didn't take much water with her brandy and so you were limited in the amount you could add. When you made the coffee, however, you had no such restrictions. All you needed to do was make sure the cup and brandy glass were back in the kitchen, washed and put away, before anyone noticed what you'd done. I would suggest it was also you who unlocked the front door that morning as a way of diverting attention."

"Of course I didn't." Mrs Harris was on her feet. "Why would I want to murder the woman who had given me a job and home for the last five years? I was grateful for everything she did for me." She addressed everyone in the room. "I had no motive, none whatsoever, and I don't know what this tincture is you're talking about."

Eliza took a deep breath and glanced at the inspector.

"Thank you, Mrs Thomson. That was very helpful. Now, I'd like us to turn our attention to Mr Robins. When we first arrived this afternoon, there was confusion about his presence. As he correctly stated, he'd never met Mrs Milwood and we have confirmation he was in Over Moreton at the time of her murder. So why is he here?" The inspector gestured for Eliza to continue.

"During the investigation, we learned that Mr Robins and Mrs Harris have been walking out together for the last six months."

Mr and Mrs Wilson gasped and turned around to look at their cook.

"Mr Robins works as a gardener for a respectable house in Over Moreton and a little over a month ago, the cook at the residence announced she was leaving. This presented a perfect opportunity for Mr Robins. He'd had his eye on the married quarters for some time and so, knowing they were available, he asked Mrs Harris if she'd marry him while at the same time taking up the position of cook."

The sound of murmuring in the room caused Eliza to pause before Inspector Adams called for quiet.

"Thank you, Inspector." Eliza's eyes rested on the vicar. "Tell me, Vicar, as the only person in the room who doesn't look surprised by this, am I right in thinking Mrs Harris came to see you about a marriage ceremony on the afternoon of Mrs Milwood's death?"

"I … erm…" The vicar glanced across at Mrs Harris but she failed to meet his gaze.

"So the rumours were true?" Ruby's eyes were wide as she stared at Mrs Harris.

"It would appear so," Eliza said, "but there was a problem, wasn't there, Mrs Harris?"

"I don't know what you're talking about." Mrs Harris refused to acknowledge that Mr Robins was in the room but he jumped to his feet and hurried to her side.

"I can't stand by listening to this. Mrs Harris is a decent and charming woman…"

"Mr Robins, please. Could you let Mrs Thomson finish?" Inspector Adams said.

Mr Robins nodded and patted Mrs Harris on the shoulder and returned to his seat.

"Please continue, Mrs Thomson."

"The problem was, when Mrs Harris told Mrs Milwood of her intention to leave, Mrs Milwood wouldn't accept her resignation. Although she always complained about her, it seems she thought rather highly of her. She said so in a letter to Mr Robins' employer."

The colour suddenly disappeared from Mrs Harris' usually rosy cheeks.

"But you knew this, didn't you, Mrs Harris?" Eliza said. "You visited Mr Robins' employer on several occasions to ask them for the position but unfortunately, because of their friendship with Mrs Milwood, they refused to change their mind. You last spoke to them the day before Mrs Milwood's death."

"How could I call the day before her death? It was a Tuesday..."

Eliza cocked her head to one side. "That's a very good question. You had no reason to be in Over Moreton that day, but it wasn't the only Tuesday you were there. When I called yesterday to speak to Mr Robins, the two of you were together in the garden. Mrs Petty saw Mr Robins arrive to collect you and later bring you back in a carriage."

Mrs Harris glared at Mrs Petty. "You nosy busybody..."

"Enough please, Mrs Harris," the inspector said.

"I was only doing what any good neighbour would do." Mrs Petty sat up straight and folded her hands in her lap.

Eliza watched them for a moment before continuing. "Mrs Harris, I suspect you were angry when you returned from Over Moreton the afternoon before Mrs Milwood died, weren't you? You'd once again been turned down for the position in Over Moreton, but you weren't going to let someone like Mrs Milwood stop you from having a husband. As soon as you arrived home, you stormed into the garden and ripped the leaves off several foxglove plants. You pretended to Mrs Wilson they were comfrey leaves, and she had no reason to doubt you given the similarity between the two. Only a trained gardener, doctor or apothecary would reasonably be expected to know the difference."

Eliza turned to Mr Robins. "And that's where you come in, sir. Had it not been for you pointing out the differences between the plants, I suspect Mrs Harris wouldn't have known the toxic effects of the foxglove."

"Don't you come over all high and mighty to me." Mrs Harris stood up and strode towards Eliza, pointing her forefinger at her. "You think you're the only one who knows these things, but I've been a cook for over forty years and I know the difference between foxglove and comfrey. How do you think I've avoided poisoning everyone for all these years?"

"So it was no accident that you walked to the back of the garden to find the foxglove leaves, rather than picking comfrey from by the kitchen door."

"You don't know I picked those leaves."

"What I do know is that Mrs Wilson saw you picking leaves that you later told her were comfrey. The problem is that at the time, she was sitting in the window seat of her bedroom and you can't see the kitchen garden from there." Mrs Harris' face was scarlet as she glared at Mrs Wilson.

"But that's not all. I've seen the way the foxglove leaves were torn from the stems of the plants and noticed the rash on your hands. You even came to the surgery for a lotion to stop the itching telling Dr Thomson it was because of an extended amount of washing-up. The thing is, foxgloves can be toxic to anyone who touches them, especially if the leaves are ripped or damaged. The rash on your hands is likely to be directly related to the way you tore the leaves from the plant and crushed them before adding them to the gin."

"You can't prove that."

"If you'd like to come into the garden, I can prove that the leaves were ripped from the plants. You left plenty of evidence behind. We can also demonstrate that you have an allergic reaction to the leaves by bruising some more and applying the liquid to your skin."

Mrs Harris flinched and put her hands behind her back. "I'm not going through that again."

"So you don't deny you've already felt the toxic effect of the foxglove, Mrs Harris?" Inspector Adams stepped towards her.

"It's not what it seems. She asked me to get some for her ... I didn't know..." Mrs Harris looked around frantically as the inspector walked towards her. When she could see no escape, she sat back in her chair.

"Mrs Maud Harris, I'm arresting you for the murder of Mrs Milwood on Wednesday the thirteenth of June using a tincture of digitalis. Sergeant, can you put the handcuffs on her?"

"No, you can't do that." Mrs Harris struggled as the sergeant and constable worked together to bind her hands. "I didn't mean to kill her, I only wanted to frighten her so she'd let me marry Mr Robins. Is it such a crime to want to start a new life? You don't get many chances at my age."

"But you were prepared to let my son go to the gallows for something you did?" Judith was on her feet. "How could you? Maybe if you'd had children of your own..."

"That's enough, my dear." Eliza put an arm around Judith's shoulders and led her to the other side of the room where Mr Robins sat, staring at the commotion. The inspector followed.

"Mr Robins, I'd like you to accompany us to the station as an accomplice to murder," the inspector said. "You can either come voluntarily or we can handcuff you if you resist."

Mr Robins pushed himself to his feet and ambled towards the inspector. "I didn't know she'd kill her, I thought she was interested in plants ... and in me." His eyes glistened as he looked up at the inspector. "Please believe me, I had nothing to do with it."

CHAPTER TWENTY-NINE

Three months later

E liza closed the front door behind her as she and Connie pulled their coats more tightly around them.

"The weather's changing," Connie said as they headed to the footpath across the green. "Who'd have thought we'd be into September already?"

"And that Henry would have gone back to Cambridge? I don't know why he had to go back so soon, the new term doesn't start for another few weeks yet."

"He'll be back." Connie smiled. "He won't want to miss Christmas at home."

Eliza nodded in the direction they were heading. "It looks like the Wilsons are ready to leave. I hope it works out for them."

"I'm sure it will. With Mr Wilson now in charge of Moreton Industries, not to mention more money than they could have imagined, they've got themselves a splendid house in London. They'll be able to get themselves settled in before Flora goes off to university."

"She's a bright girl and I'm sure she'll make the most of it."

"The only disappointment is they'll miss the re-dedication of the bell tower," Connie said. "With Mr Wilson donating the rest of the money to the fund, you'd have thought they'd wait another couple of weeks."

"I don't suppose they mind after everything that happened."

"So it seems, but I for one will be thrilled to have the clock working again. I've missed hearing the bells."

Eliza grimaced. "I haven't, it's been nice having some undisturbed sleep. Still, I suppose they need to get a move on with winter approaching."

"Are you ready to leave?" Connie shouted to Judith as they approached the other side of the green.

"We are, although typically we're waiting for Frank. There was one last news story he wanted to write up before he left."

"He must be excited about moving to Fleet Street," Eliza said.

"Oh, he's delighted, as you can imagine. I'm just thankful that they're all coming with us and we'll be able to put these last few months behind us."

"And at least the trial's over now."

Judith smiled. "Thank goodness. I was angry with Mrs Harris at the time, but I'm glad they tried her for manslaughter rather than murder. At least she won't face the death penalty."

"She won't get her new job or her husband though," Connie said. "I heard the other day that Mr Robins has found a new lady to walk out with, someone from Over Moreton. I wouldn't be surprised if they're living in the married quarters long before Mrs Harris comes out of jail."

"Poor thing," Judith said.

"Poor thing! After everything she put you through," Eliza said.

"I know, but you have to feel sorry for her, don't you?" Judith said. "I probably shouldn't say this, but she did us a great favour and yet she ended up being punished for it."

"And quite right too." Eliza scowled at Judith. "Have you forgotten she'd have happily seen Sam hang to save her own neck? You can't poison someone and pretend it wasn't you, much less let someone else take the blame."

"No, I suppose not. Still, thanks to you she got her comeuppance."

Judith sighed as her son came running towards them. "Here's Frank now, talk about cutting it fine. Come on you. Go and help your father with the last of the bags."

Frank raced into the house as Eliza watched him. "Has Sam gone already?"

"Yes, he and Ruby left yesterday. The marriage ceremony will be next Tuesday and they wanted to make a few arrangements beforehand."

"Her mother will miss her," Eliza said.

"She will, but she's happy her daughter's found a husband who'll take care of her and she'll come and visit. I hadn't realised they'd been so well-to-do before she lost her husband. It's a sad tale."

Connie nodded. "I was fortunate Mr Appleton made provision for me before he died or I'd be in the same boat."

"Can I interrupt you, ladies?" It was the coachman who

was taking the family to London. "Mr Wilson thinks he's got everything but asked if Mrs Wilson could make a final check."

Judith nodded as a man carried a large crate to the carriage.

"I'd better be going. You will look out for the new owners, won't you? They should arrive tomorrow. They seem like a nice couple and they have two young children."

"I'm sure we will. After all the excitement of the summer, I'm looking forward to becoming a normal part of village life." Eliza smiled as she embraced Judith. "If I feel the need to investigate any more murders, I'll make sure they're only the ones in the newspaper."

THE NEXT BOOK IN THE SERIES

Death of an Honourable Gent

A prestigious event, a croquet mallet, and a body floating in the lake. *Eliza Thomson Investigates...*

April 1901: A weekend house party at the stately home of the Earl of Lowton ... with an invitation to his daughter's debutante ball. It should have been perfect.

And it would have been ... had it not been for the body found dead in the lake.

The timing couldn't be worse. With only hours to go before the biggest event in the Lowton's social calendar, the family have no intention of letting it ruin the occasion.

But Eliza isn't family.

Determined to prove the death was murder, Eliza enlists the help of husband Archie, and best friend Connie. But it soon becomes apparent that not everyone wants to see justice done.

Can Eliza fight against powerful vested interests and expose a killer? Or is she risking too much for the sake of her principles?

This is the third standalone story in the *Eliza Thomson Investigates* series. If you like Miss Marple-style murder mysteries, and women sleuths with attitude, you'll love this historical British series.

Available through my website at:
www.vlmcbeath.com/books/eliza-thomson-investigates/death-of-an-honourable-gent/

Also available as an audiobook.
Visit www.valmcbeath.com/audio/ for a sample and further details

OTHER BOOKS IN THE ELIZA THOMSON INVESTIGATES SERIES

Thank you for reading!
I hope you enjoyed it.

If you'd like details of other books in the series search for
VL McBeath
on Amazon or your local bookstore.

Other books include:
A Deadly Tonic (A Novella)
Death of an Honourable Gent
Dying for a Garden Party
A Scottish Fling
The Palace Murder
Death by the Sea
A Christmas Murder (A Novella)

**Further books in the *Eliza Thomson Investigates*
series are planned for 2023!**

Keep up to date with what's new, by joining my newsletter at:
https://www.subscribepage.com/eti-freeadt

or

visit my website at **www.vlmcbeath.com**

AUTHOR'S NOTES AND ACKNOWLEDGEMENTS

I've been a fan of Agatha Christie style mysteries for many years and when I started planning the *Eliza Thomson Investigates* series I knew I wanted a similar sort of setting to the Miss Marple novels.

Obviously, the character of Eliza is quite different to Miss Marple, but I wanted a village similar to St Mary Mead, the setting for a number of her books.

That was when I came up with Moreton-on-Thames. I decided it would be useful to have the village in the vicinity of London but I wanted the rural setting and the country doctor's practice for Archie. The fact that Eliza could work with him was a bonus.

It was good fun to come up with the design of the village and hopefully you have some idea of the layout after reading the book.

Once again, I must thank my husband Stuart, dad Terry, friend Rachel and fellow authors Rose and Vicky for reading various drafts of the book and giving me feedback. Without them, as well as my excellent editor Susan, I'm sure the story wouldn't be as tight as it is.

Finally, I'd like to thank you for reading. I hope to see you for the next book!

ALSO BY VL MCBEATH

Family Sagas Inspired by Family History...

The *Ambition & Destiny* Series

Short Story Prequel: *Condemned by Fate*

Part 1: *Hooks & Eyes*

Part 2: *Less Than Equals*

Part 3: *When Time Runs Out*

Part 4: *Only One Winner*

Part 5: *Different World*

A standalone novel: *The Young Widow*

The *Windsor Street Family Saga*

Part 1: *The Sailor's Promise*

(*an introductory novella*)

Part 2: *The Wife's Dilemma*

Part 3: *The Stewardess's Journey*

Part 4: *The Captain's Order*

Part 5: *The Companion's Secret*

Part 6: *The Mother's Confession*

Part 7: *The Daughter's Defiance*

To find out more visit: **www.vlmcbeath.com/**

FOLLOW ME

at:

Website:
https://valmcbeath.com

Facebook:
https://www.facebook.com/VLMcBeath

BookBub:
https://www.bookbub.com/authors/vl-mcbeath

Printed in Great Britain
by Amazon

34456922R00148